SEVEN SLEEPERS **THE LOST CHRONICLES** 5

The Temptations of PLEASURE ISLAND

GILBERT MORRIS

MOODY PRESS
CHICAGO

Contents

1

Pleasure Island

It is time for your departure," Goél said in a quiet voice that was mild and yet at the same time strong. He looked around the small dining room, and a warm light filled his eyes. He put his gaze upon each of the five young men present and then looked directly across the table to where two girls completed the company of the Seven Sleepers.

Their leader did not make a kingly figure. He was dressed merely in a simple light gray robe. The hood was pushed back from his face, and his auburn hair caught the light from the lamp that illuminated the room. He seemed as much a simple workman as anything else, yet every member of the Seven Sleepers knew that this man had powers that could not be explained in natural ways.

Josh Adams, the leader of the Sleepers, sat studying Goél's face. At the age of fourteen, Josh was tall and awkward. He was still shy, but his entire loyalty went to this one who had saved him and the others from death many times.

"Will you be going with us on our new mission, sire?"

"No, my Joshua. I have another mission, but you will find this task mostly to your liking, I'm sure. At least at the beginning."

Bob Lee Jackson, always called Reb by his friends, was finishing a drink of refreshing tea from a large mug. He was the tallest of the boys. He was fifteen and had light-blue eyes that appeared able to bore right through an object. He had removed the tall cowboy hat that he wore everywhere except when sleeping or at the table—and sometimes even then. Reb chuckled and said, "If I didn't know you better, Goél, I'd think you were joking us. We've never had an assignment yet that was just fun."

Josh knew that was true. The Seven Sleepers had come to Nuworld from the distant past. They had been placed in sleeping capsules by their parents just before Oldworld was destroyed by nuclear war. When they awoke many, many years later, they discovered that most of what they had known was gone. Life was completely different in Nuworld. But they soon gave their allegiance to Goél, who was fighting against the Dark Lord, an evil being who wanted to enslave everyone.

Goél perhaps was remembering this as he nodded. "Indeed, you have been hard pressed many times. You have not had an easy life in Nuworld. But—" he smiled quickly "—as you well know, it is the hard times that make men and women strong. Not the easy times."

"Well, then, sire," Jake Garfield put in, "we ought to be strong, because we've sure had some hard times." Jake was a short boy of fourteen. He was of Jewish ancestry, he had red hair, and he had a quick, sharp wit. He was also great at inventing practically anything that he had the materials for. Jake grinned crookedly. "I agree with Reb here. You must be teasing us."

Abigail Roberts, also fourteen, was the smallest of the Sleepers as well as the best looking. She had fair hair and eyes, blue as the sky. Unfortunately, she was somewhat proud of her good looks. Abbey said, "Is it really true, Goél? You're going to give us a *vacation?*"

Before Goél could answer, Wash Jones—the youngest Sleeper, a black boy of thirteen—grinned broadly. "A vacation! That's what I need. I'd sure like to go somewhere where all I had to do was lie on my back and catch fish and then have somebody clean 'em and cook 'em for me."

Goél laughed aloud. Josh had always suspected that their leader had a special fondness for Wash Jones. "That may be somewhere in your future, Wash. But I can understand why Jake and Josh are a little skeptical."

Dave Cooper, a tall fifteen-year-old, was handsome enough to be a movie star, if there had been any movies in Nuworld. He had light brown hair and wide-spaced gray eyes. "Lead us to it, sire," he said. "I'm ready."

Goél then looked toward Josh's close friend Sarah Collingwood.

Sarah was small and graceful. She had large brown eyes, very black hair, and was completely devoted to Goél.

"And what about you, daughter?" Goél asked. "Are you tired of fighting saber-toothed tigers and dragons?"

She managed a smile. "I think we all would welcome a vacation, sire, if you're serious."

Goél nodded and looked around at his young friends. "I am serious. I am sending you to Pleasure Island."

"Pleasure Island!" Jake cried. "Is it anything like Coney Island? I mean are there carnival rides and stuff like that?"

The Sleepers began to fire questions at Goél, and Josh noticed that he managed to avoid most of them. He finally held up his hand, saying, "You have been in hard, dangerous places, but Pleasure Island has not yet been infected by the Dark Lord." A cloud seemed to go across his features. "I do not know how he has missed it, but no doubt he will find it someday. In any case, you will like the royal family. The king and queen are friends of mine. I should tell you that the king has had some difficulty, and I am hoping that you will be able to be of help to him as well as enjoy a vacation. That is my wish."

"Is there a princess?" Dave wanted to know.

"Indeed there is. A very attractive one. Princess Cosima."

"What is she like?" Abigail asked eagerly.

"I think she's very much like . . . like Abigail. She loves to brush her hair and wear beautiful clothes."

Everyone giggled at this, and Abbey herself blushed. "We'll be good friends, sire." She nodded vigorously. "I just know we will."

"I trust that you will, indeed. Now—" Goél removed an envelope from a pocket. "Give this letter to the king. He will give you a good reception, I am sure."

Josh, being the leader, was always trying to think ahead. "You mentioned a problem with the king that maybe we can help with. What is the problem? Is he sick?"

"No," Goél said slowly. "He is healthy enough. Very strong and athletic in fact."

"What is it, then?" Josh asked.

"He is subject to fits of discouragement, I'm sorry to say," Goél told them sadly. Then he straightened his shoulders and added, "But he is a good man. He belongs to the House of Goél, and you will find him kind, I'm sure. Now—" he got to his feet "—come. The ship awaits."

In a short time the Sleepers were standing on the

shore beside a beautiful ship with the name *Eagle* on the side. The sails were furled, but the sailors stood ready to set them as soon as the passengers were on board.

"You will have a safe voyage, my young friends." Smiling, Goél went around and shook hands with each of them. He also looked deeply into the eyes of each one.

His gaze somehow made Josh feel that he was being searched. He supposed they all felt that way.

It's always like that, he thought after their leader had shaken his hand and looked into his eyes. *I feel as if he looks right down to the inside of me and knows what's going on. Makes a fellow uncomfortable sometimes. But, knowing Goél, you know he means only good.*

The Sleepers boarded, and the captain—Captain Leland, they learned—said, "Your baggage is all aboard. Are you ready?"

"Let's go, Captain. Take us to Pleasure Island!" Jake cried.

The captain shouted, "Weigh anchor! Hoist sails!"

Very quickly the *Eagle* caught the breeze and sailed out of the harbor. The Sleepers all gathered in the stern of the ship and watched Goél as they swiftly moved toward the sea. He grew smaller and smaller, and Josh said with a sigh, "I wish he were going with us, Sarah."

"So do I." Then she reached over and poked Josh's arm. "But we're going to have a great vacation. Our first vacation in Nuworld."

The voyage on the *Eagle* was pleasant. There were no storms, and day followed day, filled with bright sunshine and a brisk warm breeze. The Sleepers enjoyed their sea voyage thoroughly.

Jake even rigged a line and managed to hook a shark, which nearly pulled him overboard.

"Let go of that line!" Josh screeched and made a grab for Jake as the shark was tugging him over the rail.

"That's my shark!" Jake yelled back.

Josh pulled his friend's hands loose from the line just in time and watched it disappear in the sea.

"That thing would have you for lunch. Let's bait up again. Maybe we can catch something that's both good to eat and safe to catch."

Later they did indeed catch a fine marlin, which proved to be good eating.

The ship was comfortable, but it was small. By the time Captain Leland alerted them with, "Land just off the port bow!" Josh—and everyone else—was eager to set foot on land again.

The *Eagle* drifted into a beautiful harbor.

"Look at that beach!" Josh breathed. "Nothing but white sand as far as you can see."

"It was like this on the beaches in Florida back in Oldworld," Abbey said. "My family and I used to vacation there every summer. And see, there are lots of people out on the beach getting tans. I can't wait! I want to get the best tan I've ever had!"

But Josh turned to Sarah. "You'll have to be careful, Sarah, and so will I. You remember how badly we sunburned when we were in Trabango? And you don't even burn easily."

"Yes, I sure do remember," she said. "We don't want any more of that."

The crew made the ship fast to a dock, and the Sleepers soon stood wishing farewell to their captain.

Captain Leland looked around with envy. "Wish I could stay with you. Pleasure Island. Sounds like a good place to be these days."

"Why don't you stay, Captain?"

"Under orders from Goél. Got to do my duty. But you youngsters have a great time. From what I hear, you deserve it."

After the farewells, Josh looked around him and said, "I guess we'd better find our way to the palace. Let's shoulder this gear."

"Can't we hire someone to carry all this?" Abbey said. "We're on a vacation!"

"You're right. We'll do that," Josh said.

Soon he had hired a man with a large cart pulled by a sturdy horse to haul their equipment. "We need to get to the palace. Do you know the way there?"

"Indeed I do. This way, sir."

They started inland and soon were all exclaiming over the beauty of Pleasure Island.

"This is a beautiful place!" Dave marveled. "Beautiful trees, beautiful sky, the homes are nice, the people are so attractive."

"A little different from what we usually find," Reb said. He suddenly said, "And look at these horses coming!"

Two riders swept by, sitting on the backs of unusually beautiful horses.

"I bet they'll win a race or two in their time," Reb said with admiration. "I'd sure like to straddle a horse again."

"Well, maybe you can play cowboy here," Jake said. "I'd like to see what kind of science they've got going on Pleasure Island."

"And I'd like to know if they have parties and things like that," Abbey said.

They made their way steadily onward, led by the helpful man with the horse and wagon.

Josh was walking with Sarah. "Have you noticed all the posters that we've been passing, Sarah?" he asked after a while.

"I have. They seem to have a lot of sports events on Pleasure Island, don't they?"

Indeed the walls of most buildings they passed were covered with announcements of all sorts of athletic contests. There were horse races, ball games, and even some sporting events that Josh had never heard of.

"They certainly do believe in games in this place," he said.

"And parties and musical events too. I've seen half a dozen notices for balls and concerts and plays and things like that."

Dave came up to walk with them just then. He was grinning. "So this is Pleasure Island. It beats having to fight a T-rex before breakfast."

Josh remembered. The Sleepers had been in lands where they had to battle dinosaurs and, even worse, sorcerers and magicians skilled in the dark arts. Pleasure Island was definitely better.

Then they arrived at the palace. They stood before a magnificent building that rose at least five stories toward the sky. It was spread out over large grounds and was surrounded by a low alabaster wall. Inside the wall were gardens and fountains, and young people everywhere were engaged in various games. Some were playing tennis. Others were hitting a golf ball around. Play, Josh decided, was the order of the day on Pleasure Island.

When they reached the front gates, Josh went up

to a guard, who was dressed in white and scarlet. "I have a letter for His Majesty King Leo."

"If you will come into the reception hall, I will see if the king is available."

The Sleepers followed the attendant and soon were wandering about an elegant room. It was filled with beautifully constructed furniture, colorful pictures hung on the walls, and lights gleamed everywhere. They were served refreshments without being asked if they wanted any. The snacks consisted of a delicious cool drink that no one could identify and small cakes that melted in the mouth.

"I could get used to this in a hurry," Reb said. He took another swallow of the drink and said, "This is even better than Pepsi!"

The attendant came back, smiling. "The royal family will receive you. If you will come this way, please."

The Sleepers left the large reception room and followed the man down a wide hallway. It made several turns before they came to a door attended by two more guards, also in red and white. They swung open the doors, and the Seven Sleepers marched in.

They all gasped. This room made the other seem small by contrast. It stretched out in every direction. And there before them, seated across the room, were four people.

"I have your letter from Goél." The speaker was obviously the ruler. "I am King Leo," he identified himself. "And this is my queen, Tamsin." He gestured then to a beautiful young girl with blonde hair and blue eyes. "This is my daughter, Princess Cosima. And my son, Prince Derek."

Cosima looked about fourteen and Prince Derek possibly twenty. All of the family was attractive.

As leader, Josh spoke first, saying awkwardly, "You'll have to forgive us, Your Majesty. We don't know how to behave in the presence of royalty. Do we just bow or do you wish us to kneel?"

"Neither is at all necessary. You come as friends of Goél. That is sufficient. For state occasions we might show a little more formality. But come, sit, and we will have refreshments. We appreciate your visit, and we want to hear about your adventures."

Soon the Sleepers were all seated, and indeed the royal family did seem interested in hearing everything about them.

Prince Derek seemed to study them thoughtfully, but he said little for a time. When he did speak up, he said with a smile, "We've heard much about the Seven Sleepers, and I must admit I expected someone older."

Josh grinned. "People always say that. Well, we will be older someday."

The prince grinned. "I hope you will have a long stay with us. By the way, I'm entered in a race today. I would like it if you would be my guest in the royal box."

"A horse race or a footrace?" Reb asked quickly.

"A horse race, as a matter of fact. Are you interested in horses?"

"He's the best horseman you've ever seen, Prince Derek," Sarah said.

"Indeed! Well, that touches my pride! We shall have to look into that. Perhaps he and I could have a private race."

"We'd be glad to join you in your box, Prince Derek," Josh said quickly.

"And tonight there is a ball." Princess Cosima was beaming. "You all must come. It is going to be absolutely fabulous. There will be many young people and music and entertainment."

"Oh, but we can't come!" Abbey said with disappointment written all over her face.

"Why is that?" the princess asked, surprised. "Have you other plans?"

"We didn't bring any party clothes! I don't have a single long dress—nor does Sarah."

"Oh, is that all? That is easily taken care of!" Princess Cosima looked relieved. "We can have the royal tailors fit them, can't we, Mother?"

"Certainly! It will be no trouble at all. And they are swift workers."

"Then it is all arranged," the princess said. "Now, girls, come with me. We shall talk about what kind of dresses the tailors can make up for you in a hurry."

An attendant showed the boys to their quarters, and each of them was given a private room. As usual, however, they managed to get together in the sitting area to talk about their situation.

"This is about the best thing I've run into since I won the bronc-riding contest in Texas," Reb said. He looked around at the luxurious room and sighed. "What a relief! No problems. No dangers. Just have fun."

Josh found himself tremendously relieved. He was tired of responsibility and tired of tension. He expelled a breath and flopped into an overstuffed chair. "You're right about that, Reb. Looks to me like we're going to have a great time here on Pleasure Island. No dragons, no dangers, nothing but fun and games!"

2

The Cat Climbing Contest

The arena was the most magnificent structure that the Sleepers had yet seen in Nuworld. It was of light gray marble and was built in a circle.

"This looks like the pictures I saw of the old Coliseum back in Oldworld," Josh said.

The Sleepers were settled in the box reserved for the king and his family. As Josh looked around, he saw that the huge stadium was packed with people in brilliant clothing. Below, a racetrack ran around the outer edge of the arena floor, and green grass grew in the middle.

"Looks like a big football stadium," Jake said. "Well, they sure take their sports seriously here."

Sarah and Abbey were much more interested in the large royal box than they were in the actual floor of the arena. For a time they wandered about, escorted by Princess Cosima. The king and queen apparently were not coming, but the princess seemed delighted to show them around.

"We have any kind of refreshment here that you like," the princess said. She nodded to a white-coated attendant, who smiled back at her. "Just ask for it, and you can have it."

"Do you have any hotdogs?" Sarah asked with a little smile. She knew full well that they would never have heard of this delicacy.

The attendant frowned in puzzlement. "Hotdogs? I'm afraid I don't know that one, miss."

"It's what they used to call a kind of sandwich a long time ago," Sarah said with a glance at Abbey. "Do you have any lemonade, then?"

The attendant listened as Sarah described lemonade. Then he brightened. "We have something very much like that." He quickly concocted a drink, filled a glass, and handed the icy beverage to her. "I hope this suits you, ma'am."

Sarah tasted it. "Delicious!" she said. "As good as I've ever had."

As Sarah sipped her drink, Abbey was talking excitedly with the princess. "I'm so thrilled that you asked us to the ball! What sort of occasion is it?"

The princess looked puzzled. "Occasion? It's . . . a ball."

"Well, I mean," Abbey said, "is it to celebrate something? Is it a special event?"

Cosima laughed at that. "Every ball is a special event."

"Do you have them often?" Abbey asked.

"Oh, not too often. Sometimes three or four days will pass without a ball."

"Three or four days!" Abbey was astonished. "I've never heard of so many balls."

"Is that many?" Princess Cosima seemed truly puzzled. "How often do you have balls where you come from?"

Abbey muttered, "Well, we haven't had any at all lately. But back where I used to live—in Oldworld—we might have what you would call a ball once or twice a year."

"Once or twice a year!" Cosima appeared stunned. "That's terrible! How did you live between balls?"

"Oh, we managed," Abbey said. "But I like it better

the way you do it here on Pleasure Island. I'm so anxious to see the dress that your tailors are making for me."

"We'll leave the arena early—as soon as Derek wins his race. I'm sure you'd rather look at dresses and shoes than to watch horses running around in a circle. Although Derek is awfully good at it. We're all very proud of him."

Down in the lower level of the arena, Reb Jackson stood beside the prince, who was stroking the nose of a beautiful mottled-gray horse.

"This is Thunder," Prince Derek said. The horse suddenly nipped at his hair, and he dodged. "Now, now, I'm not an apple for you to bite on!" he said. He laughed and ran a hand over the silky mane. "He's never lost a race—which means I have never lost a race since I've had him."

"He's some horse," Reb said with admiration. "Don't know as I ever saw a finer one."

"I'll tell you what we can do, Reb. Tomorrow we'll go to the stables. There's a horse there that I think you would like very much. The only trouble is that he's difficult to handle. Not many can stay on his back, but . . ."

"Well, that's my kind of horse!" Reb said. He felt excitement well up inside him at the very thought. "I wouldn't want a horse that wouldn't put up a fight every time somebody tried to get on his back."

"You certainly won't have that trouble with Lightning," the prince said, grinning. "He tries to pulverize every rider. As a matter of fact, there are only two men that can ride him. Myself and one other."

"Better make that three," Reb said with a nod.

Derek clapped him on the shoulder. "Well, come on. Let's go upstairs and join the rest of the family. I'll introduce you to Lightning tomorrow."

The two of them started climbing up to the level where the royal box was located.

"Hello. I won—as you saw," Derek said.

Everyone crowded around the prince, telling him what a magnificent ride he had made. He shrugged them off with a grin, saying, "It all depends on the horse. I have the best. And now it's about time for the cat-climbing contest. I want to see that."

"About time for *what?*" Josh exclaimed, not believing his ears.

"The cat-climbing contest." Princess Cosima smiled brightly. "Don't you have that in your world?"

"Not that I know of." Reb scratched his head. "What is it?"

"Come over here," Prince Derek said. "I'll show you." He led them to the edge of the royal box, where they could look down on the arena. "See? They have the climbing poles already planted."

Josh and the other Sleepers looked downward. Six poles rose some twenty feet in the air. They looked like large telephone poles to Josh. On top of each was a small platform with something placed on it.

"What's that on top of the poles?" Dave asked. "I can't make it out what it is."

"Oh, that's the food. Goodies for the cats," Princess Cosima said.

"That's the only way they get fed. They're trained that way," Derek explained. "And they're kept quite hungry just before a contest like this."

"You mean they have a race to see which cat can get to the top first?" Josh was amazed.

"Exactly! I can't believe they don't have this kind of competition where you come from?"

"Never heard of such a thing," Josh murmured. "Is it a timed contest?"

"Oh yes. The first cat to reach the top and the food is the winner. The poles have been oiled to make the climbing more difficult."

"The cat climb is a very important event today," Princess Cosima said. "The betting is high."

"Did you put down a bet, Cosima?" her brother asked.

"Yes, but only a thousand finnigs."

"Uh . . . *finnig?* Is that what you call your dollars?" Josh asked.

"I suppose so," the prince said. "If dollars are money."

"And you bet a thousand of them on a cat climbing a pole, princess?"

"I do usually bet more," Cosima said. "But it's going to be a close contest. I wasn't quite sure."

"I looked at the odds," Derek said. "I picked Black Diamond. He's had a good season."

As they watched, the cats were brought to the foot of the poles by their owners and held there. The princess and the prince continued to talk about their climbing qualities. Josh listened to them, totally astonished.

"They just look like big alley cats to me—lean and muscular." Reb murmured. "This is funny. They talk about those cats as if they were horses."

By now Josh was feeling stunned. He whispered to Sarah, "They do take their sports seriously on

Pleasure Island. Anybody that would bet on a cat climbing a pole would bet on anything."

"Time for them to go," the prince announced. "Now let's see who's the champion. This is only the semifinal, though," he added. "The grand championship will be next week."

"Yes, I'm planning to bet a lot of money on that," the princess said.

The cat-climbing contest was not particularly exciting to anyone in the royal box except the prince and the princess. But Josh watched as, at a given signal, the cats were released and began scrambling up the poles. The crowd went wild. He looked at the princess. She was screaming and waving her arms.

Leaning toward Wash, he said, "There's something wrong with this place. Anybody that would bet on *cats* like this has to be crazy."

"Black Diamond won!" Cosima cried. "I won, and I'm going to collect my winnings! Now I just wish I had bet more. Come with me, Sarah. You and Abbey come with me."

The girls left, and the boys stayed with Derek. Other contests would follow, Derek said, including footraces and wrestling.

"I guess you have just about every kind of sporting event there is, Prince Derek," Jake said.

"We do like our sports on Pleasure Island. They are very important to our people. They take sports seriously."

Too seriously? Josh wondered.

Down on a lower level, the girls approached a row of elevated cages. People were lined up before them, receiving money.

"Just stay with me," Cosima told Sarah and Abbey. "We'll soon have enough money to do anything we want to for the rest of the day."

Sarah watched the princess collect her winnings, all in coins. She put them in a large white leather bag and turned around, triumphant. "Now, let's go spend it!"

Sarah was not as excited about this as Abbey was. For one thing, she had been watching a poorly dressed man standing by one of the nearby pillars that supported the upper levels. What caught her attention was his face. It was as pale as ashes. Then another man spoke to him, and Sarah heard, "What's wrong, Garold?"

"I lost it all! I lost everything! I bet on Raffles. Everything I had."

"Never mind. There's another race. You can bet again and win it back."

"But I have nothing left to bet! I gave my house for security. Now I can't pay for it. My family and I will be out on the streets."

The second man drifted away, after muttering a few words of comfort.

"Look there, princess," Sarah said. "That poor man lost everything he had."

"What's that?" Cosima said absently. She gave the man a careless look. "Oh. Well, of course, somebody has to lose. Otherwise, it wouldn't be any fun. I lose myself sometimes."

"I don't think that's quite the same thing," Sarah said thoughtfully.

"Whatever can you mean?" Cosima stared at her with astonishment. "Of course it's the same. I lose. He loses."

"I mean that you're very wealthy. And if you bet and lose, you can just go to your father to get more money. But that poor man's lost his house."

"Oh, I understand that. But there's plenty of work. He can work and save up and buy another house."

Sarah stared at the beautiful girl with astonishment. Cosima had not seemed to be a heartless person, but Sarah saw that she was totally blind as far as the poor man's plight was concerned.

Sarah decided she would risk telling Cosima what she thought. "It seems to me that your people take gambling so . . . seriously."

"It's just good sport!" Cosima cried. "Didn't they have things like this in your world?"

"Yes, they did."

"Well, it's all the same, then. It's just for fun."

Sarah did not agree that the gambling part was just fun, but she said no more.

"Come, girls. Let's go shopping," Cosima said gaily.

And shopping they did go. For the next two hours, Sarah and Abbey were taken on a whirlwind tour of shops. The princess could not spend her winnings fast enough. She bought seven pairs of shoes.

Sarah was amazed. "Don't you have any shoes?"

"Oh, certainly. I have more than three hundred pairs."

"Three hundred pairs! Then why do you need more?"

The princess appeared bewildered that she should ask. "Oh, I don't know. Some people collect some things, and I collect shoes."

From then on, Sarah watched in silence as the princess spent all the money that she had won. She had boxes of clothes and shoes—including some she had bought for Sarah and Abbey.

Abbey, of course, was terribly excited. She whispered, "Isn't this wonderful, Sarah?"

"It's wonderful for the winners," Sarah said quietly.

"I can't wait to put on my new clothes. That ball is going to be fabulous."

The ball was indeed fabulous, if fabulous meant expensive parties. Josh stood to one side with Wash and Reb, watching the activity. The ballroom was packed with young people and older people as well. The women's bright dresses—reds, yellows, greens, blues—made a kaleidoscope of color. The music came from orchestras that were posted high on balconies. It appeared to Josh that all the Sleepers were stunned by the lavishness of it all.

"This is some set-to, ain't it, now?" Reb marveled. "I been to two county fairs and three snake stompin's," he remarked, "but I ain't ever seen nothing like this."

Wash had just come back from the refreshment table, and he had both hands full. "I don't know what all this stuff is, but it sure does taste good! It's all free too."

"No, I don't think it is free," Josh said. "Somebody's got to pay for it."

"Well, the king pays for it, I guess."

"And where does the king get the money to pay for it?" Dave asked with a crooked grin.

"Never thought about it," Wash said.

"He taxes the people."

"That's right," Josh put in. "So no matter whether the people are here or not, they pay for these fancy balls."

"Looks like they have some kind of special entertainment coming up again," Dave said.

This time it was a juggler, who was marvelous indeed. He kept at least twenty balls in the air at the same time. At other times he threw lighted torches and caught them, seemingly with ease.

Following this there was a short play, then more dancing.

"This is just wonderful, isn't it, Sarah?" Abbey had been conversing with a tall, blond-haired young man.

Sarah said, "I can see it's going to be very tiring. We'll be ready for bed tonight. Early."

But they did not get to bed early. Food continued to be brought in, the entertainment continued, the ball went on, and it seemed as if it would go on until morning.

Finally Josh found Sarah and said, "I can't take any more of this, Sarah. I'm falling to pieces, I'm so tired."

"So am I."

"We'd better pull our people out of here."

"I expect you're right. From what the princess said, there'll be another day at the arena tomorrow—and another party tomorrow night!"

"They've scheduled events I never even heard of," Josh groaned. "Even worse than cat climbing. And these people bet on everything!"

Josh soon found that all the Sleepers were ready to go except Abbey. She protested, but he insisted. "Tomorrow's another day, Abbey. There'll be another ball to go to—I'm afraid."

"Isn't this exciting! There's always something going on! This is the best place I've ever been, Josh!"

Josh looked at her and then over at the merry-makers. He sighed. "I think a thing like this could get old very soon."

Abbey looked back at him as if he had said something insane. "Get old! Why, I would *never* get tired of it if I lived to be a hundred!"

"We'll see," Josh said. "Now, let's go get some sleep. We're all worn out."

3

Another Side of Pleasure Island

The sun beat down upon the three figures lying on towels on the white sand. All three appeared to be asleep. The gentle sound of the surf lapping close to them was soothing. They had been up late every night for two weeks, and Sarah had finally suggested to Josh, "Let's go down and just lie on the beach and do nothing."

"I'm for that," he groaned. "This entertainment life is wearing me out."

Surprisingly, Abbey had chosen to go with them. She and Dave had thrown themselves full speed into the life of Pleasure Island. Maybe even she needed a rest.

Abbey stirred herself and sat up. She was wearing a pretty light blue swimming suit. It was new. She studied her arms carefully. "I wish I would tan quickly like you do, Sarah. I'm so fair I have to take the sun in little doses."

Indeed Sarah, being a brunette with darker skin, had gained a golden tan in the few days that they had been here.

Josh envied her. "You don't burn quick like I do," he said.

Then they all sat up and just enjoyed the quietness of the beach for a while.

Suddenly Abbey exclaimed, "That's going to be a great party they're planning for tonight. The princess says so. Everybody's going to be there."

"Oh no, not another one!" Josh groaned loudly.

"Why, Josh, of course there's going to be a party. We've been talking about this one for days."

He flopped back on his towel. He threw his hand over his eyes to shade them from the sun and then muttered, "There's such a thing as partying too much, Abbey."

"You're talking to the wrong person, Josh." Sarah stretched out on her stomach and, putting her head to one side, studied Abbey.

"Well, I think the two of you are wet blankets!" Abbey said, and she pouted a little. Then, shading her eyes with her hand, she watched a pair of sailboats that appeared to be racing, and then she remarked, "What was all that talk you gave Goél about wanting to get away from dragons and saber-toothed tigers and danger?"

Josh knew that he had, indeed, made such a statement. "Well, I do appreciate not having enemies and having to get up to do battle every day, but . . ."

"And now you don't like it when everything is fun. You're never satisfied, Josh!" Abbey tossed her head. Her lovely blonde hair fell down around her back, and she stroked it for a moment. "I've got to get my hair done in a different way. Sarah, let's go look at some clothes."

"Look at clothes! We've got more clothes now than we'll ever wear. The princess has just showered us with them," Sarah protested.

"Well, I'm going! Sure you won't go with me?"

"No. I'm just going to stay here and soak up the sun and the quiet," Sarah said sleepily.

Abbey picked up her towel and bag and walked away.

For a long time neither Sarah nor Josh said a word. And then Josh said, "You know what, Sarah?"

"What now?"

"I'm tired of parties."

"Me too, Josh. And I'm tired of races."

"And you know what else? I'm starting to think that Goél sent us here for more than a vacation or even helping the king. I'll bet he wants us to learn something by being on Pleasure Island."

He squinted his eyes against the sun and studied a flock of white birds wheeling overhead. "This is a great place, but these people think about *nothing* but having fun. Everybody goes somewhere every night. A party, or a race, or a concert, or a ball. There's got to be more to life than just having fun!"

The two lay there quietly for a while longer. Then Josh added, "I'd like to do something just . . . simple."

"That's what I'd like to do. But Dave and Abbey, they're really into this kind of life."

"I know. Wash says the people here are frantic. They never slow down."

"Where's Reb anyway?"

"Have you forgotten? He's working with that stallion Lightning."

"Oh, I did forget! He's in that big race this afternoon. Wearing the princess's colors."

"I think he's long gone over her."

"I don't know about that, but I'm sure she really likes him. I don't think she's ever met anybody like him before."

"How do you mean?"

"Oh, you know. She's the princess, so everybody is half afraid of her. Even the boys that like her act that way."

"I guess so. I know I was always afraid of pretty girls." He grinned and poked her with his toe. "Like you."

"You didn't show it when we first met! You were awful!"

"I still am." He grinned and prodded her with his toe again. "There. See how awful I am?"

"Keep your old toes to yourself!" Sarah sat up and put on her sunglasses. "But you know how Reb is. He just comes right out with whatever is on his mind. He treats the princess just like she was any other girl."

"That could get your head chopped off in some places."

"She likes it, though. She's never been treated like a real girl before. Always like somebody on a pedestal."

"Well, Reb likes the horse racing, but he's not much for the princess's parties."

"I know. And it drives Princess Cosima crazy. She wants him to go to every one, and he just won't do it. I think it's the first time she's ever told somebody to do something and they wouldn't do it."

"It's good for her. Might give her some humility." Then Josh said, "I've got to get out of this sun. I'm starting to cook."

"I'm ready to go," Sarah agreed.

After they went into the dressing rooms and changed back into their street clothes, Sarah said, "My bow needs some work done on it, Josh."

"Nothing Jake can fix?"

"Oh, if I could get him to stay still long enough he could fix it. But Prince Derek told me about a family named Fletcher. They live over on the edge of town where the working people are. Derek said he's great with any kind of weapons. I'm going over and have him take a look at it."

"Mind if I come along?"

"Not a bit. Let's go."

They picked up Sarah's bow and, a half hour later, arrived at a shop that had the name *Fletcher* over the door. The sign had an arrow stuck into it, as if to emphasize the profession of the owner.

"I guess this is the place," Sarah said. "This part of town isn't quite as fancy as the palace area, is it?"

Obviously they had reached the part of town where the poor people lived. The houses were small and jammed next to each other. The children who played in the street were not dressed in fine clothing as children were in other parts of Pleasure Island. A pair of them now, a boy and a girl no more than three, sat studying them as they approached. They were sitting in a mud puddle and apparently had been giving each other mud baths.

"Hey, I'd like to try that!" Josh said. "Come on, Sarah. Let's give it a whirl!"

"Take your grubby hands off me, Josh Adams! If you want to sit in the mud, go ahead!" However, Sarah was charmed by the children. "Aren't they cute?"

"You think every kid's cute. They look like muddy kids to me."

Josh and Sarah walked into the shop.

A tall man with salt-and-pepper hair was working at a bench. He got up at once and bowed. "Yes. May I serve you?"

"I am Sarah Collingwood, and this is Josh Adams."

"My name is Jacob Fletcher." He studied the bow in Sarah's hand. "You, perhaps, need your weapon repaired?"

"Yes. You see, a crack has started here, and I'm afraid it's going to spread."

Mr. Fletcher took the bow and examined it. "This is a fine bow," he said. "As fine as any I've seen. But it does need a little work."

"Will I need to leave it and come back?" she asked.

"No. It will not take long. Please be seated."

Instead, Josh and Sarah wandered around the shop while they waited. They picked up weapons of different kinds and commented to each other on how finely they were made. It was a small shop and was crammed with longbows and crossbows. There were daggers, swords, and shields.

Josh was impressed. "Mr. Fletcher knows his business," he said quietly, "but he's not rich."

"No, he's just a workingman. And it's kind of a relief to see one of those. We've seen so many pampered rich people lately—people with lots of time to do nothing."

Josh grinned. "That's what you get for hanging out with the king and his family."

At that moment a little girl came in. She was perhaps six years old. She had dark hair and very dark eyes, and she smiled at them. "Hello," she said.

"Well, hello. What's your name?" Sarah smiled back.

"My name is Lalita."

"This is my daughter," Jacob Fletcher said proudly.

"Papa, Mama says for you to come to eat."

"You tell Mama I'm working right now."

"Oh, don't let us interrupt your lunch," Sarah said quickly. "We can wait."

"Mama said to bring your customers in. That she has enough for everyone."

"My dear, I'm not sure they would like to eat in a humble place like this. You're welcome, of course," he said, turning back to Josh and Sarah.

"We'd be glad to share a meal with you, Mr. Fletcher," Sarah said at once.

"It's not like the palace," he warned. "Just very plain food."

"Sounds good to me," Josh said. "I'd give anything for just a plain bowl of soup and a piece of bread, Mr. Fletcher."

"Well, you can have that, I'm sure. And you may call me Jacob. Come along into our living quarters."

They followed Jacob into the kitchen, where they met his wife and their son, Mark. Mrs. Fletcher was a strong looking, plainly dressed woman with brown hair and brown eyes. She sat them down to a good but simple meal.

Josh was impressed by the looks of Mark Fletcher. He had a rather spectacular build. He was only nineteen, his mother informed them, but he was a champion wrestler.

"He has beaten everyone," Jacob said, gazing proudly at his son.

"I may not beat the next one though, Father." Mark was well over six feet and powerfully built. He wore a light cotton shirt and a pair of simple brown pants.

Josh thought his eyes would surely bug out looking at the young wrestler. The muscles of Mark's arms were enormous. When he had a chance, he whispered to Sarah, "He looks strong as an ox."

"But he's nicer looking than an ox! The whole family's nice," she whispered back.

"Do you get paid for wrestling in the arena, Mark?" Josh asked.

"He will not take money," Mr. Fletcher said rather proudly. "The professionals have tried to hire him, but he refuses."

"Why is that, Mark?" Sarah asked curiously.

The young man smiled rather shyly. He had a nice smile and warm brown eyes. "I think that takes the fun out of it. I'd rather wrestle just because I want to."

"Some very wealthy men have tried to sponsor Mark. They know they could make much money by betting on him," Mrs. Fletcher said. "But we think it is better that he doesn't. We think all this gambling is very bad."

Josh and Sarah exchanged glances. Josh remarked, "I'm surprised that you feel that way. It looks to us like everyone bets on Pleasure Island. Of course, we haven't been here long. Only a couple of weeks."

"You are right, though," Jacob Fletcher said. "Almost everyone does gamble. But not quite all. Not I, myself. Most of our neighbors do. And those who can least afford it gamble the most, it seems."

"That's true." Mrs. Fletcher ladled more soup into her husband's bowl. "I don't know when it all started. When I was a girl, there were games and contests—but not so much betting on them."

"I think the king gets a part of all the bets that are made," Mark said. He frowned. "I enjoy wrestling just for the sport, but I have a friend who has gone absolutely crazy about it. Wrestling is all he can talk about. You can't carry on a conversation with him about anything else."

"I've known people like that." Sarah sighed. "Not about wrestling particularly. But people get interested in a hobby or a sport or something else, and—as you say—they are impossible to talk to about anything else."

"It is a bad thing," Jacob said. "Several of our friends have trouble with their youngsters. They don't want to work. They want to do nothing but play."

36

"Pleasure Island," Josh murmured. "That's what they call the place, and I guess that's what it is."

Jacob Fletcher scowled. "It is no pleasure for those whose children have gone mad about having fun. It is no pleasure to those men who lose all they have and are thrown out of work."

"I saw a man like that the first day we were here," Sarah said. "He had borrowed money on his house and lost it when whatever he gambled on lost. What will happen to him?"

"He will work in the mines," Jacob said shortly.

"The mines? What are the mines?" Josh said.

"It is a place for people who have lost everything. They work from daylight to dark for practically nothing."

"They're more like slaves than anything else," Mark added. There was sorrow in his eyes. "Several of our friends and neighbors have wound up there. We tried to talk to them about how dangerous their gambling habit was, but they wouldn't listen."

They finished the simple meal, and then Jacob finished repairing Sarah's bow. He named a price, and Sarah paid him. But she protested, "That's not enough, Jacob. And you even entertained us for lunch!"

"It is enough. Honest pay for honest work."

"I'll hope we'll see you again," Josh said as they prepared to leave.

"You must go and see my son wrestle. Then we shall see each other. He is indeed amazing. The best on the island."

"Well, I'm tired of most of the things at the arena, but I would like to see that," Sarah said.

"Good. It would please Mark if you would go. He wrestles tomorrow at two o'clock."

37

Josh and Sarah started back toward the palace, and Sarah said, "They are such a nice family."

"They are. Real friendly. And real sensible."

"It's good to see that there are some level-headed people around here who haven't gone sports crazy or are gambling away everything they have."

Back at the palace, they found the prince and the princess waiting for them. For some reason, both looked unusually serious.

"Is something wrong?" Josh asked Derek. "Someone ill?"

Derek nodded and said rather worriedly, "It's our father. He's not feeling well today."

Cosima seemed troubled, too. "He has these times when he's absolutely discouraged, and of course that depresses the rest of us."

At that moment Queen Tamsin came in, and Derek asked, "How is he, Mother?"

"Not much better, but he says he has heard of a physician on the mainland who is supposed to be very good with troubles like this."

"Has Father sent for him, then?" Cosima asked.

"He has. And has also offered a large sum of money to make sure that he comes at once."

Josh felt awkward listening to this family talk. He almost said something, but then decided it was not his business. Later, however, after the queen left, he said to the prince, "Derek, I'm wondering if part of your father's trouble might not be the pace of life around here."

"What are you trying to say?" Derek asked, looking truly puzzled.

"Well, everybody goes so fast and furious and thinks of nothing but being entertained. That's enough to depress anybody after a while."

Derek nodded. "Yes, I have thought something along that line myself."

But Cosima cried, "Don't be ridiculous, both of you! Having fun can't make people discouraged and unhappy!"

Josh did not answer, but he was not convinced. Later he said to Sarah, "Princess Cosima might be a bright young lady, but she doesn't know much about people. You look in the king's eyes, and you can see how tired he is."

"Maybe this new doctor will help," Sarah said hopefully. "In any case, I hope so."

4

The Doctor

The massive room Lady Maeve entered was gloomy indeed. The darkness seemed to reach out and seize her, and she stood still, looking about the murky interior. So enormous was the room that the darkness blotted out the outer edges, and when she looked up she could not see the ceiling.

"Lady Maeve, come closer."

The hollow voice echoed throughout the mammoth chamber.

As Lady Maeve moved forward, her eyes fixed on the flickering light ahead of her. She was aware of strange-shaped and huge forms on each side of her. They were alive, she knew, and fear came over her, but she masked it, as she had well learned to do.

And then she was standing before a great throne on which the Dark Lord of Nuworld sat. To his right sat a woman dressed entirely in black, who watched her with glittering eyes.

"I have come at your command, my lord," Lady Maeve said.

"You have performed well in the past," the Dark Lord began. His voice was smooth and somehow deadly.

Far overhead in the ceiling, lightning ran back and forth, and Maeve caught the sound of faint screams that chilled her to the bone. However, she gave no indication of this but merely bowed. "Thank you, my lord," she said in a strong voice. She had learned to conceal

her fears, but the eyes that bored into hers were difficult for her to meet.

"I have a mission of some importance for you. If
you succeed, you will be richly rewarded. If you fail—"

"I have never failed, my lord."

Laughter issued from the mouth of the Dark Lord,
and he glanced at the woman beside him, who had not
taken her cold eyes off Lady Maeve since her arrival.

"No, as yet you never have, and that is why I have
sent for you."

"What would you ask of me, my lord?"

The Dark Lord suddenly stood. He loomed over
Maeve, who waited before him in the semidarkness. He
did not move further, but she somehow felt power
emanating from him. Indeed, his power seemed to fill
the entire cavernous throne room.

He appeared to be waiting for her to speak, and
when she did not, he said, "Good. You are a woman of
strength. Very well. Here is what you must do. As I say,
rich rewards will be yours once you have succeeded."

"I am yours to command, my lord."

"Then listen. I would have you leave at once . . ."

The cheers of thousands filled the arena. Reb
Jackson leaned forward and urged on the mighty white
horse to even greater speed. Then he drove Lightning
across the finish line, yanked the white Stetson off his
head, and let out a wild cry of victory.

Reb had become a favorite with those who came to
the horse races. Aside from the prince himself, he seemed
to be the most popular horseman in the kingdom.

Now he pulled up the white steed, slipped off his
back, and handed over the reins to one of the horse
handlers. He petted the horse's steaming side, and

Lightning tried to nip him. Reb laughed. "That's all right. You can bite if you want to. You ran a good race."

Then Reb advanced to where a small platform had been built. This was where the awards and trophies were given each day.

Princess Cosima herself stepped toward him and extended her hand.

Reb had been coached by one of the palace advisers that, when either the queen or the princess presented the award, he was to kiss her hand. He felt rather foolish doing this, but, bending forward, he performed his duty.

And then Princess Cosima reached for the small box that an attendant handed her. "And this is for you, my Reb."

Reb took the box from her hand and opened it. His eyes widened, and he gasped, "That's the prettiest ring I've ever seen!" After that, he could only stare at the gold ring with its large green stone and wag his head back and forth. "I never even had a ring before."

"Put it on. See if it fits."

Reb took the heavy ring from the box and slipped it on the ring finger of his right hand. "Fits like a glove," he said cheerfully.

"I'm glad. It will remind both of us, every time we see it, of your great victory on Lightning. Now, remember, there is a banquet this evening to celebrate all the winners."

The princess began walking from the arena, and Reb walked beside her. He looked up at the stands, which were packed with people still screaming his name, and he grinned. "Seems like a big to-do over a horse race."

"You've become very popular, Reb. Everyone in

the country knows who you are. How does it feel to be famous?"

"Doesn't feel like much of anything except that my ears get tired when everybody yells like that."

Cosima took his arm. "You are a strange young man! Most boys would love to be famous."

"It's all right, I guess. And I got me a green ring out of it." He held up his hand and admired the ring again. Then he looked down at the princess. She was especially beautiful today, he thought. She was dressed in a sparkling blue-sequined dress, and her hair was done in a braid that formed a wreath around her head. Her eyes were bright and blue.

Cosima said, "Do you want to know a secret?"

"Sure."

"As you know, the crown always provides the awards. But that valuable ring won't cost my father anything."

Reb looked again at the stone. "It looks expensive."

"It *is* expensive. But I bet that you would win, and you did. I had to give odds at three to one, but I won."

"Three to one! What if you had lost?"

"But I didn't lose," the princess said. "Come on, Reb. Let's get ready for the banquet. I can hardly wait to show you off. After all, you are my champion."

That night's banquet was held in one of the several banquet rooms. But this time the banquet was rather small, as such things went. No more than thirty people were present, all close friends of the king.

The king himself sat beside Lord Denning, who was Master of the Council. Denning was an older man with silvery hair and penetrating gray eyes. It had not taken the Sleepers long to discover that Lord Denning did most of the actual work of running the kingdom. The king himself was too busy with balls and races and contests.

The food was excellent, as always, but Sarah found herself looking at the king. "He looks tired, Josh," she whispered. "And really not very happy."

"He sure does. He looks downright depressed to me."

"The others in the royal family say he didn't used to be like this when he was a younger man. That just in the last year or so he's been falling into these discouraged periods."

The food began to be passed around again. There were exotic dishes such as grilled hummingbird. Each one of the tiny creatures would make a single bite. Sarah noticed that none of the Sleepers tried eating hummingbird.

"I always liked hummingbirds," Jake said. "I wouldn't feel right eating one."

"Of course, I like cows too," Reb said, "but you don't see me turning down a steak."

"That's not quite the same thing!" Jake protested.

"Why isn't it the same thing?"

"Because hummingbirds are beautiful, and cows aren't."

Reb put his fork down. "Who says cows aren't beautiful? *I* think cows are beautiful."

Laughter went around the table, and Princess Cosima said, "But you wouldn't want to eat a horse, would you, Reb?"

More laughter circled the table, and this time Reb grinned sheepishly. "You got me that time, princess. No, I sure wouldn't."

When the dinner had been going on for some time, an attendant dressed in purple came in and whispered in the ear of Lord Denning. As soon as he left, Lord Denning said loudly enough so that Sarah could easily hear him, "Your Majesty, the physician from the mainland is here."

The king drew a hand across his face. His eyes still had a troubled light, and he sighed. "Well, he will do little good, but admit him."

Queen Tamsin leaned over and put her hand on her husband's arm. "You must be hopeful, dear," she said. "This doctor comes very well recommended."

All eyes turned to the door, and there was a surprised murmur as the doctor entered.

Sarah—and probably everyone else—had been expecting a doctor with white hair and spectacles. Instead, a beautiful young woman entered. She was dressed all in black and had black hair and black eyes. There was a confident air about her as she marched into the banquet hall. She went directly to stand before the royal couple and bowed deeply, rather than curtseying as a woman usually would.

"Your Majesty, I am Lady Maeve. You sent for me."

The king appeared confused. He ran a hand over his hair doubtfully and said, "I was not aware—" He could not finish and seemed embarrassed.

"You were expecting a man." Lady Maeve smiled. "I am accustomed to that, Your Majesty. I learned my skills from my physician father. He is too old to make this sort of journey anymore, so he sent me in his place. I hope you are not displeased."

The king shook his head. "I really have little hope of help from any physicians."

"That is a condition that I hope to change, Your Majesty," Lady Maeve said.

"I suppose you will want to examine me."

"I would like to have a conference with you at your convenience, sire. I would like to know more about your problems."

"Very well. I suppose now will do as well as any. Excuse me, my friends."

The king rose, and, of course, everyone rose with him. He and the new doctor left the room, and conversation buzzed around the table as people reseated themselves.

"Wow, I think I'm getting sick," Dave said. "Never saw a doctor who looked that good."

"Me too. I don't feel well at all," Jake moaned. He held a hand to his forehead. "I think I'm getting a temperature."

Abbey glared at them. "That's no way to carry on! This is serious!"

Prince Derek turned to his mother. "I was surprised that the doctor proved to be female. But perhaps, if she knows her business, she will be a help."

"We'll hope so, my son."

The king proceeded down the hallway toward his study, followed by Lady Maeve and a servant. The servant opened the door, they went inside, and he turned to face the new doctor.

"What will you require?"

"Just a little privacy while we discuss your problems, Your Majesty."

"You may go." The king dismissed the servant and sat down.

Lady Maeve sat opposite the king. "Your Majesty,

it is very important that a patient have confidence in his physician. You do not know me, so I cannot ask for that yet. But I will ask that you keep an open mind."

The king looked into the clear eyes of the young doctor. They were so black that they seemed to have no pupil. A strange fragrance drifted from her—not perfume exactly but something much like it. He shrugged his shoulders and said bitterly, "It would be better, Lady Maeve, if I had an ailment of the flesh. We have excellent physicians here, but who can minister to a diseased mind?"

"I hope to do exactly that, Your Majesty. Now, this may seem rather foolish to you, but would you mind if I burn a little incense while we talk?"

"Incense!" The king looked at her strangely. "Is that part of your treatment?"

"Partly," Lady Maeve said with a smile. "In my research, I have come upon a secret ingredient that seems to have a soothing effect. I often use it myself when I'm troubled."

Immediately the king's interest was aroused. "Well, indeed, I would be most gratified if it would succeed."

Lady Maeve reached into the bag that she carried and quickly set up a small incense burner. It was no bigger than a large cup, but when she lit the flame underneath it, the room was soon filled with a strong but not unpleasant odor.

"Pay no attention to the incense, Your Majesty," Lady Maeve said lightly. "Soon it may relax you a little, and that is all I am interested in at the moment. Now tell me your symptoms."

The king sat back and began to speak. "I've always been healthy in body," he said, "but of late I have become depressed."

"How long has this been going on?"

"A year or two. Maybe three. It came on very gradually."

"And you have no physical ailments?"

The king laughed. "No. I'm very strong for my age. Very healthy indeed."

As the conversation went on, the king found himself indeed relaxing. The doctor had a smooth, gentle voice, and the smell of the incense did have a soothing effect. In fact, he talked longer than he normally would. Finally he said, "I find that you are easy to talk to, Lady Maeve."

"Thank you, Your Majesty. I hope so. And now I think I may have very good news for you."

"You mean you can help me?"

"I believe it is possible." Lady Maeve reached into her bag again and drew forth a crystal vial filled with a ruby-colored liquid. "This has been successful with some of my patients who have had your very symptoms."

"What is it?" King Leo asked. He felt growing excitement.

"It is the juice of a very rare plant that grows only in one area of Nuworld. So far as I know, it has never been cultivated successfully away from that one place. I call it Soma."

"It looks harmless enough. What does it do?"

"It has a soothing effect for most people. But those who are depressed find that it works just the opposite for them. It seems to cheer them up, strange as that may seem."

"Ah, that would be wonderful." The king sighed.

"Shall we try it, then?" Lady Maeve smiled winningly.

"Yes, indeed."

"Then we will have a glass of wine." She arose and took a container from a table. She filled a small goblet and carefully added a single drop of the ruby-colored liquid. She swirled its contents, and said, "Drink this, sire. And I think you will find yourself feeling much better very soon."

King Leo took the goblet. He held it for a moment and looked into its crimson depths, then lifted it to his lips. He drank it all, wiped his lips with his handkerchief, and nodded. "We will see, Lady Maeve, whether you are a physician or not."

Lady Maeve took the cup from the king's hand. A satisfied look flashed for a moment in her eyes. She smiled and said quietly, "Yes, sire, we shall see. And very soon."

5

A New King

Josh leaned against the wall of Jake Garfield's room, watching him work on a new type of sword harness. Jake was always trying to improve things. "I haven't heard much out of you lately, Jake," Josh said idly. "What have you been up to?"

Looking up from his work, the redhead grinned. "I've been trying to convince Prince Derek to let me become chief inventor for Pleasure Island. I think I—" Jake never finished his sentence.

Abruptly the door opened, and, to Josh's astonishment, King Leo himself walked in.

"Your Majesty!" Josh exclaimed. He came off the wall and straightened up at once.

Jake scrambled to his feet, and both boys bowed.

"Well, well, what is this? Two young men just standing around doing nothing? I came to call you. We've got to be on our way!"

Josh blinked, bewildered. "On our way to where, Your Majesty?"

"Why, to the arena, of course. I told you about it at breakfast. Or did I?"

The king's eyes were bright, and the pupils looked enlarged. His hair was ruffled where he had apparently run his hands through it. Then he asked impatiently, "Where are the rest of your friends? I can't find them. We're going to be late!"

Josh had truly forgotten that the king had said something about attending the afternoon games. He had no intention of saying so, however. Instead he said, "Sure. Come on, Jake. His Majesty's waiting."

"I'll get the other guys," Jake offered. "What about the girls?"

"They're already on the way with the princess. Now, hurry along."

Jake quickly rounded up Wash and Dave and reported that Reb had already gone to the games with the princess. Then the four boys hurried along toward the arena, well behind the king and his attendants.

On the way, Prince Derek joined them. He was shrugging himself into a jacket.

"What's your father in such a rush about today, Derek?" Josh asked in a low voice.

Giving Josh a harried look, Derek shook his head. "He's been like this for days now. Ever since that doctor came here. Whatever she's doing has sure changed my father."

"I've noticed he's awfully busy acting," Jake said. He was puffing to keep up. "But that's good news, isn't it?"

Derek did not answer for a moment. "I suppose so," he said dubiously. "But it's such a turnaround."

"You mean so much better?" Josh questioned.

"No, I mean . . . true enough, he was depressed before, and we worried about that. But now he gets up and starts in from sunup to late at night. He's got to be at every play, at every ball, and he bets unbelievable amounts on the races and other events."

"Well," Josh said hesitantly, "at least he's not depressed."

"He isn't. But he's not himself, either. My father was always a steady man. Always steady. Now I never know what he's going to do next."

There was no time for more talk, for they arrived at the arena and took their places in the king's royal box. Reb and the two girls were already there. So were Princess Cosima and her mother.

"Well, well, let's get started with the games," the king said. He laughed heartily and slapped Wash on the back so vigorously that the boy nearly collapsed. "You're going to see something today, my boy. Indeed you are!"

Trying to get his breath, Wash asked, "What is it, Your Majesty?"

"It's a championship wrestling match. I have a man in my court who has defeated everybody he's wrestled. His name is Leander. If he wins his match today, he'll be the undisputed island champion." He turned then and said feverishly to the queen, "How much do you think we should bet, my dear?"

"Well, I don't think we should bet much, Leo. We don't know Leander's opponent."

"Not bet much!" King Leo's eyes gleamed, and he laughed loudly. "We're going to win a fortune on this. Here, Derek." He reached down to his belt and brought up a large, heavy leather sack. "Go bet all of this on Leander."

Derek hefted the sack, and he blinked. "But Father," he said, "there must be several thousand finnigs here."

"Right! And there will be that many more. You'll have to give odds, but put it all down. Two to one if you have to."

"Oh, this is so exciting, Father!" Cosima cried. She drew out a smaller bag and said, "Bet this for me, too, Derek."

Derek took both money sacks, but he frowned. "I don't like to do this," he said.

"Oh, don't be such an old fuddy-duddy! You're too

young for that." The king laughed loudly again. "Go on now, son. Do as I tell you. You'll see. We're going to win a bundle."

With a despairing look at his mother, Derek turned and left the royal box.

Josh could see that the queen was agitated but that Cosima was highly excited.

"I don't think this is working out too well," he murmured to Sarah.

She did not have a chance to reply, for at that moment Lady Maeve entered the box.

At once the king said boisterously, "Well, it's my physician. Come, my dear. Sit here with the queen. You can see the action very well from here."

"And how are you feeling, Your Majesty?" Lady Maeve asked.

"Never felt better in my life!" the king exclaimed. "Never better! I feel like a young man again."

"You *are* young, Your Majesty. Young and strong. You should live to be a blessing to your people for many years," the doctor said smoothly.

"Lady Maeve," the queen said nervously, "the treatment that you are giving my husband. Is it safe?"

"Oh, certainly, my lady! I wouldn't think of giving the king anything unsafe!" The doctor sounded shocked to be asked such a question. "Are you unhappy with the result?"

"Of course she's not," King Leo said. He put his arm around the queen and hugged her. "She wanted me to get out of my discouraged state, and I've certainly done that."

"Yes, you have. And as your physician, I'm very pleased."

"Now then," the king said. "Let me tell you about

this wrestler Leander. He only has to defeat one young man—and an amateur at that. I'll have the champion wrestler in my stable."

"What's the name of Leander's opponent?" Josh asked.

"Mark . . . Mark something. I forget what."

Instantly Josh and Sarah exchanged glances. Josh looked quickly down at the arena. Sure enough, coming out into the competition area even now was Mark Fletcher.

"It's him," Josh said. "It's Mark. He's wrestling the champion."

"I thought Mark wasn't a professional," Sarah whispered back.

"I did, too." He raised his voice and asked the king, "You say the young man who is wrestling Leander is not a professional wrestler?"

"No, the more fool he. He refuses to take money. Says he wants to stay an amateur. Well, he'll have to stay an amateur after this." Again King Leo laughed heartily. "Leander, I fear, is a rather cruel man. He broke the neck of his last opponent. Purely by accident, of course."

Sarah drew in a deep breath. "Surely he wouldn't do that to an amateur."

The king seemed feverish. "Can't help it if he does. Can't help it if he does. I've bet money on Leander. I told him to get rid of his opponent as quickly as possible."

"Josh, maybe we ought to go down and somehow warn Mark," Sarah whispered.

"It's too late. Look, they're squaring off."

The two wrestlers below, each stripped to a pair of

trunks, began circling each other. Leander was much the larger man. He towered over Mark Fletcher.

"He must weigh three hundred pounds!" Reb exclaimed. "Mark doesn't have any business wrestling him."

"He is doing this of his own free will," the king insisted. "Throw him, Leander! Throw him!"

The action began very quickly. It was clear that Leander was accustomed to easy victories. He launched himself at the younger man, no doubt expecting to throw him to the mat, where he could pin him easily.

Instead Mark Fletcher ducked under his grip and grabbed the wrist of the big man. With a quick twist he threw the champion over his head. Leander hit the ground flat on his back. He was such a large man that the blow made a distinct thud that was heard throughout the arena. A groan went up, for Leander had seldom been thrown.

The champion scrambled to his feet and stood glowering. The muscles on his body swelled, making his opponent look almost small.

"He's a monster!" Josh whispered. "He can kill Mark if he gets angry."

Indeed Leander seemed to have that in mind. He advanced with eyes blazing. Around and around, the two men circled. Leander seemed more cautious now, however, having seen the skill and the speed of the younger man.

"Look at Mark. He's *laughing*. He's enjoying this," Sarah said.

"He won't be wearing that smile long," the king growled. His face was flushed. He was standing now, shouting encouragement to his favorite.

The match seemed to go on for a long, long time. Again and again, Leander sought a grip, but Mark Fletcher would usually evade his hands. If he did fall into the hands of the huge wrestler, he had skill enough to break free.

On the other hand, Mark was unable to throw the wrestler to the mat again.

"He's got him now!" the king screamed. "He's going to break his neck! I've seen him do it before."

"Calm yourself, dear," the queen begged. "To get so excited is not good for you."

"The king's lost his mind," Jake murmured. "He's not like himself at all."

And then Josh saw that, down below in the arena, Leander finally had both hands on Mark. His head was now caught in the crook of Leander's mighty forearm. Slowly Leander exerted his strength, and the boy seemed to be collapsing under the weight of the enormous wrestler. It became obvious that the champion was trying to snap his neck.

"Call off the match, Father!" Derek shouted. "He'll kill the young fellow!"

"He knew the risk he was taking!" the king cried. His eyes were bright and wild as he cried encouragements to his champion.

"I can't stand to watch this," Sarah said, and she turned away.

But suddenly, by some maneuver too quick for the eye to see, Mark reached over Leander's shoulder. He grabbed him under the chin and began forcing his head back. It was a struggle, but slowly Leander's head went back . . . back . . . back.

"He's got him!" Reb yelled. "He's got him!"

Mark had broken Leander's hold and now had his

own hold on the wrestler's arm. He bent it back, with the other hand pulling down, and soon Leander's shoulders were flat on the ground.

"Mark wins!" a voice cried.

And although most people groaned—they had no doubt bet against the boy—Josh saw Jacob Fletcher standing by the edge of the field, cheering for his son.

In the royal box, the king muttered angrily at his favorite. "Calls himself a champion! Bah! Bring that young man over here!" he commanded.

The master of the arena must have called Mark, for he soon came to the royal box and bowed before the king. "My victory is dedicated to you, sire," he cried happily.

"You did well. Unfortunately, you lost me a wagonload of money," the king said, "but you'll be in my stable from now on."

"But, sire, I'm not a professional. Nor do I wish to be."

"But you will become one. Not many young men get a chance to become the king's favorite."

Mark looked very unhappy. He started to protest further, but the king said, "No more of it. Report to the trainer of the wrestlers."

After Mark left, Josh managed to slip away from the others and went down to have a word with him. He saw the young man speaking with his father and went to him at once. "Congratulations, Mark."

"Thank you, Josh, but what am I to do about the king? I don't *want* to be a professional wrestler."

"Surely the king will understand that," Josh said.

"I don't know. He seemed very set on it." Mark was glum. "I wish I'd never wrestled."

Looking over at Mark's father, Josh said, "It's too bad, isn't it, that it can't be just for sport?"

"It's this betting. That's what does it. Betting makes maniacs out of people," Jacob Fletcher grunted. He too was unhappy, and he showed it. "No good will come of it," he muttered. "No good at all. You'll see."

It was the day after Mark Fletcher defeated Leander that Lady Maeve approached the king with a new thought. They were talking in private, as was their custom, and once again she was burning incense.

"King Leo," she said, "is it not unfair of you to withhold happiness from your family?"

"What? Who? I?" The king was truly surprised. "What are you talking about, Lady Maeve?"

"I mean that Soma has done so much for you, and it would do as much for the other members of your family."

"But the other members of my family are not depressed, are they?"

"No, but they are unhappy in many other ways. You, perhaps, don't see it, Your Majesty. You have been so busy with your kingly duties. But I think it's my duty as a physician to urge you to see that your whole family is on this medication."

"Medication," the king muttered. He thought long about it. Lady Maeve spoke so persuasively that finally he said, "Indeed, I think you may have something. I'll see to it immediately."

Later that same day, when the royal family were having a private meal, King Leo said, "I have something good in mind for the entire family. You have noticed the improvement in me since Lady Maeve came and put me on medication."

"Indeed, Father, you are so much more lively now," Cosima agreed.

"Well, all the credit must go to the doctor and to the medication Soma."

"The drug that she gives you."

"It's a *medication*, not a drug, Derek!" the king snapped. "In any case, I have decided that we shall take it as a family."

"I'd rather not, Father, if you don't mind," the prince said.

"I would rather not either, Leo," the queen said.

A family argument began, and in the end only Princess Cosima agreed to take Lady Maeve's medication.

The king was highly displeased with his wife and son. "You'll come around to my way of thinking sooner or later. See if you don't."

For some reason, things did not seem right in the royal household. Reb noticed a troubling change in the prince, and one day he asked him, "What's the problem, Derek? I can tell that something's wrong."

"It's my father," the prince said. "He's changed completely."

"He sure seems lively enough now."

"Lively! He is betting money as if it were water. He wants my mother and Cosima and myself to go under the care of that doctor, too. I wish the woman had never come here! And now, as of this morning, Father has gone half crazy."

"What's he done?"

"You haven't heard?" Derek exclaimed bitterly. "He's put that woman on the king's council."

"On the council! What does she know about running a kingdom?"

"Not one thing!" Derek muttered. "But she's got

my father so tied up that he doesn't know what he's doing. Reb, I don't know what to do. He wants all of us to take that Soma. So far my mother and I have refused, but—"

"Good for you. What about the princess?"

"Oh, she was happy enough to agree to it. She spent some time with Lady Maeve, and now she's happy as a clam."

Two days later, as Josh and the other Sleepers were going by the council room, the prince came striding angrily out. He looked very upset.

"What's the matter, Derek?" Josh asked.

"Do you know what he's done now? Do you know what he's done?"

"What who's done?"

"My father." Derek looked at the Sleepers and rubbed his forehead in frustration. "He's commanded all the *council* to begin taking Soma."

"What did they say?"

"What do you think they would say? All except Lord Denning agreed at once."

"The Master of the Council. What did Lord Denning say?" Sarah asked.

"He advised against it. But everyone else all fell into place. I think they're all afraid of Lady Maeve."

"Now, I think Lady Maeve is all right, Derek," Abbey declared. "After all, see how she has helped your father."

"No, I don't think she's helped," the prince said. "I think there's something wrong with that woman. Oh, she smiles, and my father's not depressed anymore. But he gambles more than ever. And he does irresponsible things like this." He looked down at his feet and then said quietly, "I don't mind telling you that I'm worried sick."

He turned abruptly and walked off.

As the Sleepers looked after him, Abbey said, "He'll come around. He just hates change. That's all."

"I don't think so," Josh said. "And I think he's absolutely right. I think that woman is . . . evil. I think there is something badly wrong with Lady Maeve, and I think the king's going to pay for it."

6

Lady Maeve's Plan

"Oh, come, Reb, you'll enjoy it!" Cosima pleaded.

Reb was at the stables, where he was brushing down Lightning. He intended to take him out for exercise. Cosima had just asked him to attend a concert with her that evening.

Reb kept on brushing the glossy hide of the stallion, who once again playfully tried to bite him. Reb lightly slapped him on the nose with the brush. "You missed me that time. He got me on the shoulder the other day, though. I've got black-and-blue marks."

"But why do you even let him try to bite you? Can't you whip him?"

"Whip him? No. He's got spirit. I like that, princess. Wouldn't have a horse without it." He grinned widely. "There's some people told me I have a little of that item myself."

"Oh, you do, Reb! And that's why I enjoy your company. I want you to come to the concert with me."

"Aw, princess, there's been a dozen concerts lately. You know I went to two or three of them, and they're all just alike."

"Not this one. This one will be different."

Reb continued to brush the stallion, but at last, being a good-natured fellow, he agreed. "All right. I'll go—but I'm not promising I'll stay long."

"Oh, you'll like it, Reb, I'm sure! It starts at seven o'clock. I've got a new dress that you'll just love."

"Well, I don't have a new outfit, but I'll clean off my

Stetson pretty good." Reb had continued to wear his high-crowned Stetson, which set him apart on the whole island. Besides, everyone knew him for his horse racing abilities. Whenever the Sleepers went down the street, he was greeted. "I'll just clean off my hat," he said.

Reb was getting ready to go off to the concert with Cosima when Josh came in.

"I see you're all cleaned up and have your hair slicked back," Josh said. "And is that a new shirt?"

"Oh, I guess so," Reb said. "Thought I'd get one after all."

"It looks good. If you drop dead, we won't have to do much to you to get you ready for the burying."

"Aw, come on, Josh! I'm going to a concert with Princess Cosima."

"I thought you hated those things," Josh said.

"To tell the truth, I don't like 'em much. But she asked me, and it won't hurt me to go one more time, I guess."

Reb met the princess, and they made their way to the building where the concert was being held. When they stepped inside, Reb stopped in his tracks. "What's going on here?" He had to yell to make himself heard. "It looks like a riot."

"Everybody's just having a good time, Reb."

"Having a good time! They look like they've all gone nuts!"

Cosima laughed and acted very excited. She said, "We'll go down close to the front where you can hear the music better."

"I don't need to hear it any better," Reb protested. Nevertheless, he allowed her to lead him through the crowd.

Since Cosima was the princess, a way opened up before her. As a result, Reb soon found himself seated in front of the platform, where six young men were playing different instruments. Reb decided that all of them had wild looks in their eyes.

"Those fellows are high on something." He shouted to be heard.

"But don't you love the music?" she shouted back.

Reb listened for a time. "Can't make anything out of it," he yelled.

"They're the very latest! Everybody's crazy about them. Look, the lead's going to sing!"

The lead indeed did sing, but Reb could not make out much tune.

"Back in Oldworld, he couldn't get a job with a three-piece band in the middle of Oklahoma." But he muttered that to himself.

He flat-out refused to dance with the princess, so she accepted other offers. He hung around the refreshment table and soon decided that there was a high alcoholic content in the punch.

Everybody here is going to be stoned but me, he thought. *Don't see why they call this fun.*

Since Reb was a celebrity, however, he found many girls trying to lure him onto the dance floor. He steadfastly refused and spent most of the evening talking with the young men who wanted to talk about sports.

After several hours of this, Reb was exhausted. He found Cosima. "Princess," he said, "do you think you can get home by yourself?"

"Why, you're not leaving!" Princess Cosima exclaimed. Her eyes were bright, and she seemed highly excited.

For a moment Reb wondered if the princess was on some kind of drug herself. Then he remembered what Prince Derek had told them. Cosima had agreed to take Soma, the same drug her father was on.

Reb said, "I've had about all I can take of this. Will you be all right? I'll wait if you won't."

"No, I'll be fine, Reb. But come outside with me before you go. I want to show you something."

They wound their way across the crowded floor to the doorway, and when they stepped outside, Reb said, "Boy, this quiet sounds good."

But right away Cosima said, "See what I have, Reb."

Leaning forward, he saw that she held a tiny glass vial. "What's that?" he asked.

"It's Soma. I want you to take some of it."

"Soma. That's what you and your dad are taking."

"Yes, and it makes you feel wonderful! Colors are brighter. Sounds are better. Everything tastes better. It just makes you feel like a new person."

"To tell the truth, princess, I may not be much, but I kind of like the person I always was."

"Oh, come on, Reb! If you'd try a little of it—just one drop, even—you'd enjoy life a lot more."

But Reb shook his head. "Not me. I saw what drugs did to folks back in Oldworld a long time ago. Alcohol and drugs—they never brought anything but misery to people."

Cosima listened impatiently. "This is *medication!*"

"You can call a pig a dove, but he's still a pig. And you can call Soma anything you want to, but it's still dope to me."

Cosima suddenly slapped Reb's face. Her eyes were blazing. "Go on and do what you please! I don't care!" She whirled and went back inside.

Reb stared after her sadly. "And if that's what Soma does to folks, I sure don't want any of it."

He did not sleep well that night.

The next day Reb talked to Sarah about what had happened.

She stood holding her repaired bow. He knew she had agreed to compete in the archery contest, although not for money. She listened to his story and then said, "I'm glad you didn't take any of that Soma, Reb. It sounds like bad stuff. It surely hasn't done her father any good."

"He's not depressed anymore. That's for sure."

"No, but there are worse things than being depressed, and behaving the way he did with Mark is one of them."

"And I feel sorry for Derek. He says his father will probably try to make him take that stuff."

"He's already tried," Sarah said sadly. "And so far, both Derek and Mark have held out. I hope they keep on with it."

Late one afternoon the council met. The king felt especially nervous, and he fidgeted while Lord Denning went over the affairs of state. Lady Maeve sat at the king's left hand today. He supposed the other council members thought that was unusual. As a matter of fact, it was unusual for a new council member to ever sit that close to the king.

King Leo listened to Lord Denning go on and on. Denning was a wise man and had run the country, for all practical purposes, for several years. During the king's times of depression, he had been the strong force that had kept things in the kingdom from falling to pieces. King Leo knew all that.

But the king was impatient with him today. "Get on with it, Denning! There's a race in thirty minutes. I must be there."

"But, Your Majesty!" Lord Denning looked shocked. "There are many items of kingdom business that we need to take care of!"

"What things?"

"There are many small items and one large one. Perhaps if we could handle that large one, the rest would take care of themselves."

"Then, speak up! Speak up! Tell us what it is!" the king said impetuously.

Denning picked up a sheaf of papers. "You have in front of you the budget. If you will examine it, you will see that we are in terrible shape financially. If something isn't done, we're going to have to cut back."

"Cut back on what?" the king demanded. He felt his face reddening.

A murmur went around the table.

Lord Denning said, "Sire, this was once a land where people worked hard and played on occasion. Now they play most of the time and work only when they have to. There is only one end to that."

At once Lady Maeve spoke up. "I believe you are wrong, Lord Denning."

A mutter ran around the table this time, for no one interrupted the Master of the Council.

Lady Maeve said, "I apologize for breaking in, but it's been my experience that happy people make for a good country. The people on Pleasure Island are happy."

"They're *not* happy! They're delirious with playing games!" Lord Denning exclaimed.

The meeting became quite heated then, and thirty minutes later the king rose and walked out.

Lady Maeve followed him.

"That old fool!" the king said. Instantly he knew that was something he never would have said before. He had always trusted and respected Lord Denning. But now he was angry to the bone.

"Well, he's getting on in years, Your Majesty."

"He is. He always was old-fashioned, and he's getting worse. Imagine, too many games! There aren't enough, I say."

"Exactly, sire. Perhaps soon it might be time to replace Lord Denning with a younger person."

The king stared long at her. "You may be right at that," he said.

Lady Maeve smiled as the king left her. She had been thinking a great deal, and now she had a scheme in her mind. She asked one of the guards, "Have you seen the Sleeper named Josh Adams?"

"He is in the library, Lady Maeve."

Lady Maeve went to the king's huge library. Few people were there, and at once she spotted Josh Adams in a corner chair, reading a thick book.

"Good afternoon, Josh." Lady Maeve smiled. "Doing some study?"

The boy rose at once and closed the book. "Why, yes. Just a little, I guess. How are you, Lady Maeve?"

"Very well. Would you care to go for a walk with me? We've not yet had time to talk."

Josh Adams seemed uncertain, but then he said, "Yes, of course. It would be my privilege." He handed the book back to the librarian, and the two walked outside.

"A beautiful day," Lady Maeve said.

"Indeed it is. I went fishing this morning. Caught a red snapper that weighed ten pounds."

"I hope you'll save a piece of it for me at dinner tonight."

"That too would be my privilege. They are delicious eating."

Lady Maeve and Josh walked in the palace grounds. She thought he seemed more relaxed with her than before. That pleased her.

Suddenly he asked—cautiously, perhaps—"Are you happy with the results of your treatment of King Leo, Lady Maeve?"

Lady Maeve said quickly. "Oh, yes, but there is much to do yet. Indeed, he is out of those dangerous depressions. I don't think anyone knew how serious they were. I do think he would have taken his life if something hadn't been done to help him."

"Really?" Josh said, seeming shocked by the thought.

"Oh yes. He was getting worse all the time. His wife or his children can tell you that. His periods of depression were lasting longer."

They continued walking. The boy did not speak for a time and then said, seemingly with effort, "Well, that's serious news indeed."

"Yes, of course. But Soma is a powerful—and helpful—medication. However, it does have to be balanced. Neither too much nor too little." She looked at him thoughtfully. "I think it might be helpful if you tried Soma, Josh."

"Me? But I'm not depressed."

"Soma is not only for those who are depressed or who have mental illness," she said. "People react differently to it. I think that, with your temperament,

Soma would give you the ability to see things much more clearly."

"What do you mean, Lady Maeve?"

"I mean that with people like you, Josh, Soma clarifies the mind. You are the leader of the Sleepers, and I would suppose there have been times when you've had to agonize over what to do, what decision to make."

"You're right about that," he said fervently.

"Exactly! Then, I would suggest that you take a very small amount of Soma and see what happens to the decision-making process."

Josh was quiet again. Finally he turned to face her. He seemed nervous now. "I'll think about it," he said finally. "I've learned not to make any decisions too hastily."

"A very wise move indeed. You think about it, Josh, and I believe you'll see I'm right. Well, thank you for your time. It has been a pleasant walk."

As Lady Maeve left Josh, her mind was working rapidly. "He has a strong will. It would be difficult to lure him on." But then a smile turned up the corners of her lips, and she nurtured another thought as she walked on.

The girl, Abigail. Abbey they call her. She would be easy. And Dave Cooper. He's rather self-centered, anyway. Those two are the weak links in the Sleepers, I believe. I could convince them, without much trouble, that a little Soma would make them to be better looking or wiser or able to have a great deal more fun.

The thought pleased her, and she sang a little tune under her breath as she set out to find Abbey and Dave.

"You know what, Josh?"

"What is it, Wash?"

71

"It's Dave and Abbey. You haven't been around them much in the past few days, have you?"

"No, I haven't. What are they doing?"

Wash scratched his head and then said slowly, "They're acting funny, Josh."

Instantly a thought leaped into Josh's mind, *Lady Maeve has gotten to them. I'll bet she's got them on Soma.* Aloud he groaned and said, "Wash, if that woman tries to get you to take any drugs, don't take anything."

"She's already tried," Wash said. "But I just told her I wasn't having any." Wash's face grew very serious. "You think that's what's wrong with Abbey and Dave? She's gotten them on drugs?"

"I'm afraid it could be. Go get Sarah and Jake and Reb—we've got to talk about this."

7

Master of the Council

"I sure don't know what is going on." Josh took another bite of apple and chewed on it thoughtfully.

Sarah was swinging back and forth in a hammock. They were in one of the many gardens that surrounded the palace, and the air had a spicy smell from the flowers that grew abundantly there. Fleecy white clouds drifted lazily across a pastel blue sky above them.

A light breeze ruffled Josh's hair. He pushed it back from his forehead and looked closely at Sarah. "Are you listening to me?"

"Mmm? Oh, I'm sorry, Josh. I guess I was nearly asleep."

"I said I'm worried about what's going on around here."

"You mean about Dave and Abbey being on Soma."

Josh took another bite of the apple and spoke with his mouth full. He mumbled, "Yeah, I'm worried about them."

"Don't talk with your mouth full. It's not good manners."

"Manners!" Josh tossed the apple core at a silky long-haired dog that was passing by and hit it squarely on the nose. The dog yelped and ran off.

"Well, that's a fine thing! Now you're into mistreating animals."

"I didn't mean to hit the silly dog!" Josh said. He got up and walked over to the hammock. "Have you talked to Abbey much lately?"

"When would I talk to her?" Sarah said sleepily. "All her time is filled with running to parties and balls and what not." She opened her eyes and looked up at Josh. "Have you talked to Dave?"

"No. Well, I've tried, but he won't listen. It's amazing how they've changed over just the last few days—and not for the better, either."

Sarah got out of the hammock and smoothed her hair. "You're right about that. There's something about that drug that . . . that releases people's inhibitions."

"You mean it makes them do things that they wouldn't do ordinarily."

"That's right. I happen to know Dave has lost money that he doesn't have by betting on things. And I suspect Abbey's doing the same."

"The princess has been loaning her money. I don't know where Dave's been getting his."

"It could be from Lady Maeve," Josh said darkly. "She's taken him under her wing. They have more confidence in her than they have in me."

"Oh, Josh, that's not so!"

"It is so!" He kicked at a beautifully colored flower and knocked the head off it. "I wish we had never come to this worthless Pleasure Island!" he growled.

Sarah walked over and stood beside him. Her face wore a worried frown, but she succeeded in making her voice cheerful. "It'll work out all right, Josh."

"I'm glad you think so. The next thing you know, that Maeve woman will be running the country."

Lady Maeve watched a crisis erupt in the council meeting. The king and Lord Denning were almost in a shouting match.

"Your Majesty," Lord Denning said, "the country is

falling to pieces. Our people are doing nothing but gambling and partying. It's got to stop!"

King Leo scowled at the Master of the Council. "We've been over this before!" he said sourly. "We'll hear no more of it, Denning!"

"But if you would just look at these figures, Your Majesty—" Lord Denning waved a paper "—you would see that the kingdom is bankrupt. People are hungry. And hungry people make revolutions, sire."

"Are you crazy!" The king snorted. "A revolution here on Pleasure Island? We've never had anything like that!"

"We've never had anything like this carnival that goes on all the time either, sire."

Their voices grew louder and louder.

Finally Lady Maeve was able to catch the king's attention. "Your Majesty, I don't want to interfere—"

"Oh, go ahead," the king said grumpily. "What's on your mind, Lady Maeve?"

"We've had these meetings now for several weeks, and they always end the same. In nothing. You and Lord Denning apparently cannot get along. I would therefore suggest that Lord Denning retire and be replaced by someone more in sympathy with your policies."

Every council member gaped open-mouthed at Lady Maeve. Disbelief washed across face after face, but she knew that no one dared challenge what she had said. They all well knew that she was in the king's favor. To challenge her was the same as to challenge the king himself.

Lord Denning was gasping like a fish out of water. "Of all the impertinence! Who do you think you are, woman? You come in here a stranger, and now you're telling us how to run the country!"

Lady Maeve waited calmly. If every council member expected the king to rebuke her, she well knew they all were mistaken—about both him and the power that she had over him.

The king looked blankly at Lord Denning as confusion swept across his face. Then he cleared his throat. "I believe Lady Maeve has a point. Now, Denning, don't be upset. We will find a very important job for you to do. But after all, you are getting on in years . . ."

Lord Denning drew himself up and said stiffly, "You need not find a position for me! I do not need your charity, Your Majesty!" He arose and stalked out of the room, his face grim with anger.

Silence reigned over the council chamber, and then Lady Maeve sent an unspoken command to the king. After gazing at her as if hypnotized, he said in a halting fashion, "You will have to forgive Lord Denning, my friends. As I say, he's getting up in years . . ."

"But who will be Master of the Council?" one of the members spoke up.

"Well . . . I shall appoint . . . I shall appoint Lady Maeve to the position, temporarily at least."

A stunned silence certainly did reign then. Not a sound was made.

Lady Maeve got to her feet at once and said, "Gentlemen, this meeting is dismissed."

When the council members had all stumbled out of the room, Lady Maeve turned to the king. "I know you're disturbed, sire, but you must not be."

"He's done good service for this country, Lady Maeve. I regret its coming to this. Lord Denning has been a friend."

"Yes, of course he has. But for the good of the

country we must move on. Come, Your Majesty. It's time for your Soma."

"Yes—yes. I think I'm in need of . . . something."

As the king turned and moved heavily toward the door, a cruel smile turned the corners of Lady Maeve's mouth upward. *So. We've gotten that fool Denning out of the way, and the council is under my command. Now all I have to do is increase the king's dosage of Soma, and he will not be any problem.*

"Your Majesty, you look tired. Are you not feeling well?"

Queen Tamsin turned to Sarah and said, "No, Sarah, not unwell. But I am deeply worried. About Cosima."

Sarah was sure that this was true. Cosima had outdone herself in recent weeks. She had gotten completely out from under the authority of her father. And when her mother tried to correct her, the king would simply say, "If you would take medication along with Cosima and me, you would see how things are."

Now the queen's shoulders sagged. She leaned forward in her beautifully designed, silk-upholstered chair and began to weep. "I know queens should not weep," she said, "but I can't help it."

Sarah went to her and tentatively put a hand on the queen's shoulder. "I don't know whoever told you that, Your Majesty. A queen is a woman, and there is a time when women need to weep. You're worried about your daughter and your husband. Who would weep for them if not you?"

Queen Tamsin reached up and took Sarah's hand. "You're a comfort, dear. Indeed you are."

Sarah took a seat on a low stool beside the queen.

"We're all concerned about your husband. Two of our own number have been persuaded by Lady Maeve into taking Soma. Their behavior is so different. They're not like themselves at all."

"Exactly the way it is with Leo and with Cosima. They're just not themselves."

"Is the king still pressuring you into taking the drug, Your Majesty?"

"Constantly. Day and night. It takes all the strength I have to resist him. As for Derek, he and his father are scarcely speaking. Our family is shattered, Sarah."

"My lady, I would not give easy words of comfort. I know only a little of what your heart must be feeling. But I would encourage you, if I could." She waited until the queen looked up and then said, "Since we came to Nuworld—miraculously, as you have heard—we have been in many dangerous places. There have been times when we despaired of life itself. But we are still here. We are alive and well. And it is Goél who has kept us so."

"Goél. I wish he would come and set the kingdom straight. He was here years ago, and both my husband and I knew that he was the right man to lead this world in the fight against evil. Oh, how I wish he would come!"

"He may come yet," Sarah said eagerly. "He comes sometimes when least expected. But sometimes he lets us get in terrible shape first. I think he does it to test our loyalty and help us learn."

The queen seemed to take heart at that. "It's a relief to talk to you, Sarah. I can't talk to Cosima anymore." The worried look came back into her face. "She's seeing a lot of your friend—the boy Jackson."

"You mean Reb. Yes. They do go places together a lot."

The queen seemed hesitant. "Is he—is he *reliable?*"

Sarah laughed. "Oh yes! He's very reliable. You don't need to worry about your daughter being with him."

Relief washed across the queen's face. "Good," she said. "You can't know how comforting it is to hear that from you." Then another thought seemed to come to her, and she said, "I wonder if *you* would try to talk to Cosima. You are almost the same age. Maybe she will listen to you."

Sarah hesitated. "I've tried to talk to my friend Abbey. As you probably know, Lady Maeve has persuaded both her and Dave to use Soma."

"Yes. Cosima told me about that. She seemed very pleased."

"Well, *we're* not pleased. We think it's a very bad thing indeed."

"So do I, and so does the prince. But my husband seems totally blinded by that woman. I can't understand it."

"I'm sure it's that drug, Your Majesty," Sarah said quickly. "It's that drug that has changed people's behavior. If we could just get rid of that and get rid of her, I think things would be much better."

"Oh, I wish we could!" the queen cried. "I worried when my husband was depressed, but this is so much worse."

When Sarah left the queen's quarters, she went to find Abbey. She found her in her room, trying on new shoes.

Four pairs were out before her, and she greeted Sarah with, "Which of these do you like the best,

Sarah? I've got to make a decision quickly. My dress has to match."

"Oh, I don't know, Abbey. They're all lovely. I'm concerned about something else. I need to talk to you."

Abbey looked up with apprehension. "Now, Sarah, I do hope you're not going to give me a sermon. Josh has already been here and done that once today. He tells me that Dave and I are doing wrong by taking Soma. But Josh is the one who's wrong, you know. And so are you—if that's what you were going to say."

Sarah shook her head. "You've got to look at what's happening, Abbey. Not only to you and Dave but to the king and to Cosima."

For some time she tried to persuade Abbey that what she was doing was a great mistake. But a barrier seemed to have been built around Abbey's mind. Stubbornly she clung to her position that there was nothing wrong with taking Soma.

"It's medication, and I'm just having fun," she said. "So is Dave. And as for the king, you don't know what an awful life he had before Lady Maeve came. He was so discouraged he was about to take his own life."

"You don't know that, Abbey."

"Yes, I do!"

"How do you know it?"

"Because—" Abbey broke off.

"Because Lady Maeve told you so. Isn't that right?"

A stubborn look came to Abbey's face. Sarah had seen that look before, and she knew that further conversation was hopeless. "We've been through so much together, Abbey," she said quietly. "I just hope you think it over."

"I don't need to think it over. I know what we're doing is all right."

"Would you want to tell Goél what you're doing?" Sarah asked quietly.

She saw a flicker of doubt come to Abbey's blue eyes, but then the girl seemed to close her mind to the thought. "I don't have time to talk! I've got to get ready for the ball."

Sarah left Abbey's room, heavyhearted. She did not want to burden Josh, who was already feeling bad enough, so finally she simply went for a walk by herself.

She found herself making her way down to the poorer part of town, and eventually she came to the Fletcher house. She stepped into the shop and found Mark helping his father. "Hello. How are you two?"

Mark brightened. "All right, Miss Sarah. You're looking very pretty today."

"Why, thank you, Mark." Sarah smiled. "It does a girl good to hear a compliment every now and then."

She talked with Mark for some time, and finally then said, "Mr. Fletcher, you've hardly said a word. Is something worrying you today?"

"Nothing is wrong."

"Yes, there is," Mark said quickly. "Father is upset because I've agreed to become part of the king's retinue. I'll be wrestling for King Leo now in the arena."

"I still say it's a bad idea, son. You will see that nothing good can come of it."

Sarah started to speak, but Mark shook his head in warning. Later, when they were alone, he said, "I agreed to do it only because I was afraid that woman might do something to my family."

"You mean Lady Maeve."

"Yes, Lady Maeve. She has the king under her thumb. He does anything she says. If she were to tell him to have my family thrown into prison, he'd do it in a minute."

"Oh, I don't think he's that blinded, Mark!"

"My father is always such a good man," the young man said softly. Despair crossed his handsome features. "We're going to have more trouble. I can feel it in my bones."

Sarah left the Fletcher household and wandered the streets for a long time. She saw that the poor people seemed poorer than ever. Clothes appeared more worn, and all the citizens had a hungry look. Mark had told her that many of them had gambled away their wages, making a few rich while many went hungry.

"This isn't right," Sarah whispered. "It isn't right, and something's got to be done about it."

8
A New Game

Reb was grooming Lightning, and that was a job he always liked. It gave him pleasure just to run the brush down the great horse's back. From time to time Lightning made a grab at him, but Reb knew the horse was not really trying to hurt him. He laughed and tapped Lightning's nose.

"You rascal!" he said. "You're about as worthless a horse as I ever saw!"

When Lightning extended his lips and made a slobbering sound, Reb reached into his pocket and pulled out an apple. "You're always begging, aren't you? I'd be ashamed of myself if I was you."

He watched, smiling, as the great stallion ate the apple, and then he began the grooming again.

Wash was sitting over to one side, watching. He was eating an apple himself, with careful, small bites.

"What do you reckon a horse like that is worth, Reb?" he asked curiously.

Reb studied the stallion with a critical eye. "I don't know about these finnigs they have around here, but back in Texas he'd be worth enough to sell the farm for."

"And he belongs to the princess?"

"Yep."

"She sure likes to win, doesn't she?"

"Well, who doesn't?"

"But these people around here think winning is everything. It's a shame how some of them have gone flat broke betting on crazy things. Do you know what the latest event was?"

"I don't know. Probably pretty wild."

"They had a chicken race."

"A chicken race! Chickens can't race!"

"Well, these did—sort of. And people bet good money on them." Disgust crossed Wash's face, and he got to his feet. He came over and stood close to the head of the great stallion. He began talking to the horse. But suddenly Lightning thrust out his big head and pushed Wash in the chest with his nose.

"Hey!" Wash yelped as he went over backwards and fell into the straw.

Reb stood laughing down at him. "Be glad he didn't bite your nose off," he said.

Wash got to his feet and glared at Lightning. "I hope you lose today," he said grumpily.

"We don't lose, do we, Lightning?" Reb said, patting the stallion's nose.

At that moment a crowd of young girls trooped into the stable with slips of paper in their hands. They were all about Reb's age, and they swarmed about him, asking for his autograph.

Reb shooed them back, saying, "Don't get too close to that horse. He's not partial to women."

One of them laughed and fluttered her eyelashes at him. "Are you partial to girls, Reb?"

Reb just grinned at her and then signed all the slips. "Now, you girls scoot out of here. You're not supposed to be in the stable anyway."

"Why don't you meet me after the race, Reb? We could have a good time," a tall, dark-haired girl said and winked at him boldly.

"Can't do that. Have to take care of this horse. Now you girls get on out."

When they had gone, Wash grinned. "Well, what does it feel like to be idolized?"

"I don't care much for it," Reb said. He sat down on a bale of hay and asked, "Got another one of those apples? I gave Lightning all of mine."

Fishing around in his pocket, Wash produced an apple, and Reb took out a knife to peel it.

"The peeling's the best part! It's good for you," Wash told him.

"Aw, I always peel my apples, and I guess I always will. Now, you tend to your apples, and I'll tend to mine."

The boys sat on their bales of hay, talking companionably. After a while, Wash went back to the subject of the autograph hunters. "You really like people yelling your name, don't you? And girls coming and asking for your autograph?"

"Oh, it's all right."

Wash stared at his friend in amazement. "Well, I think *I'd* like it. Of course, I can't ride a horse like you can."

"Let me tell you something, Wash," Reb said.

He gestured with the knife until Wash said, "Don't point that thing at me. It might go off."

Reb closed the knife, and then his face grew sober. "Why do you think those girls came in here?"

"Because they idolize you, like I said."

"What do they know about me? That is, what do they really know about Bob Lee Jackson?"

"I suppose they know you're a good rider."

"That's right. And that's all they know."

"Well, what does that prove, Reb?"

"It proves that it isn't *me* they like. They just like something I do. Suppose I broke a leg and couldn't ride a horse. Would they like me then?"

Wash seemed to think hard for a moment, and then he shook his head. "No, they'd like the fellow that took your place riding the horse."

"That's right. Well, that's why I don't get real excited when they come around."

The two talked about that for a while.

At last Reb said, "Abbey told me once that those girls that win beauty contests never feel good about themselves. They don't know whether guys like them because of who they are or because they won a contest. That seems to be the way it is."

"You sure do explain things good, Reb," Wash said. "You're just a walking encyclopedia."

"Sure, anything else you'd like to know?"

Wash thought for another moment, then said, "Would you mind explaining Einstein's theory of relativity to me one more time?"

Reb jumped at him, and the two wrestled around in the straw until Wash begged for mercy.

"All right," Reb said. "Now I'll explain it to you."

Lady Maeve was meeting with the council. The king was not present today. She had told him it was not necessary for him to attend the meetings anymore.

Maeve was well pleased with herself. She now ruled the council with an iron hand. She looked around at the men's faces. They were still and washed of all emotion. She knew that she had frightened them all into submission.

"The people are getting tired of the games," she said. "The games are too mild."

"What are you suggesting, Master of the Council?"

"I'm suggesting that we make the competitions more exciting. There will be some changes made, and I will expect you to back up any move I make in doing this. It's for the good of the country. You understand me?"

A murmur of agreement went around, and Maeve said, "Then you are dismissed!"

Lady Maeve left the castle then and made her way to a gray building with no windows. Stepping inside, she narrowed her eyes, for the only light there came from lanterns. This was the prison of Pleasure Island.

The warden met her and seemed flattered that she had come. "Ah, Lady Maeve," he said. "You've come for an inspection."

"I've come to set one of your prisoners free."

The warden swallowed hard. "The king, I suppose, has signed his release?"

"I will sign the release. That should be sufficient."

"Well, yes, of course, Lady Maeve. What is his name?"

"His name is Sylvan."

The warden blinked. "You don't want to free that man!" he cried. "Sylvan is the most notorious con man on the island! He's swindled countless people out of their life's fortunes."

"I did not ask for your opinion, warden. Take me to him."

He bowed. "Yes, Lady Maeve!"

Minutes later she stood in a dank prison cell. Straw was on the floor, and the only light was a single candle. A man sat across from her—on a bed complete with a plush mattress and quilt. She stared at him intensely, and he stared back.

"What do *you* want?" he muttered.

The sorceress moved a step closer. "I want to take you out of this place, get you cleaned up, get you good food. Anything you want."

Sylvan grinned, revealing amazingly white teeth. Despite his prison uniform, he was a dapper looking man. He was well over six feet tall and had a manicured mustache and beard.

"You must want something rather important—and illegal—done to promise me that."

"And will that stop you, Sylvan, if I ask you to do something illegal and dangerous?"

"Let me out of this place—" Sylvan smiled grimly "—and I'll poison the king himself."

Lady Maeve smiled in spite of herself. "It hasn't come to that—yet. I want you to become head of the new national gambling game." She knew that Sylvan had himself operated various gambling schemes that cheated people, including animal races, sporting events, and gambling casinos.

Now the man stood up, apparently keen to hear her offer.

"What is it you want, madam?" he asked graciously.

"I want to expand on these mild little games of chance. I want the people to be offered the opportunity to bet everything, everything they own. I want to call this game 'You Bet Your Life.' If they win, they capture a great prize. If they lose, they belong to me—and the salt mines."

Sylvan, the criminal, grinned and nodded. "I'm your man, Lady Maeve. A little slavery never hurt a kingdom."

9
The Salt Mines

The Fletcher household had become a second home to Josh and Sarah. Sarah was very fond of Lalita, the six-year-old daughter, and she spent hours with her. It proved to be a relief to play simple games with the child instead of getting caught up in the whirlwind of activities that seemed to engulf the entire island.

Josh enjoyed the company of Jacob and Mark. The man was like a father to him. Jacob was kind and patient and witty, and he seemed to delight in Josh's company.

Mark undertook to teach Josh something about wrestling and was very patient with him. Wrestling with Mark, of course, was always a one-sided contest. The young man was fully developed, tremendously strong, and faster than a striking snake. However, he did manage to teach Josh a few of the fundamentals of the sport.

As the two of them were practicing one day, Mark said, "It's not strength so much as it is speed, Josh. Strength is important, of course. But the strongest man in the world would be helpless if he were trapped in a bone-breaking hold. Here, let me show you."

Josh listened carefully to his friend's instructions. Although he was aware that Mark was allowing him to control the situation, it gave him a thrill when he was able to send Mark over his head to land on the mat that they were practicing on.

"You see? And I outweigh you by seventy-five

pounds. So you could use this hold successfully on practically anyone except another professional wrestler."

They took time out then, just long enough for a short break. When they went inside the house, Mark's mother offered them some delicious little cakes she had just made. Josh happily began eating his as fast as he could.

Lalita laughed at him. "You can have all the cakes you want, Josh."

"They're just so good I can hardly stand it," he said. "I can't help gobbling."

Lalita said, "Mama and Papa don't like it when I eat like that."

"That's right. And you listen to them. Don't use me for your model, Lalita." Josh grinned at her and took another big bite. "I never did win any medals for my table manners."

Jacob Fletcher seemed to hear something then. He got up and went to the window and looked out. He exclaimed, "Why, it's our friend Feanor!"

His wife joined him at the window and said, "What in the world has happened? He looks terrible."

Raising the window, Jacob called out, "Feanor, come in!"

Josh and all the Fletchers turned to the door as the man entered. Josh had met Feanor. The man and his wife had three fine sons and a little daughter. They had eaten meals together with the Fletchers a few times when Josh was also there.

"Whatever is wrong, Feanor?" Mrs. Fletcher cried, going to him. "Is it your wife? Is she sick? Or one of the children?"

"No. It's even worse than that." Feanor groaned.

He passed a hand in front of his face, and Josh could see that it was trembling. Perspiration had burst out on his forehead, and he was a terrible ash gray color.

"Here, sit down, Feanor," Jacob said. The man seemed almost unable to obey, and Jacob had to help him into a chair. "Now," he said kindly. "What is it? Tell us. You have friends here. We can help with whatever problem you have."

"I've been a fool," Feanor groaned.

"Well, so have all of us at one time or another," Jacob said. "We all make mistakes."

"Not like this one!" He seemed unable to speak except in a feeble whisper.

"Just tell us what it is," Mrs. Fletcher urged. "There's a solution for most things. We just have to find it."

Feanor looked up then, and Josh saw a hopeless look in his eyes such as he had never seen before. He thought, *What in the world can it be?*

"I've lost everything," Feanor finally managed to tell them.

At once Jacob stiffened. "Feanor! You haven't been gambling again, have you?"

"Yes, fool that I was!" Feanor cried. "I know you've warned me about it a thousand times. I thought it was a sure thing this time. I thought I couldn't lose."

"There's no such thing as a sure thing in gambling," Mark put in. "What did you bet on, Feanor?"

"The dog races. And I talked to the owner of one of the dogs. He assured me that he couldn't lose, so I—"

He broke off, and Mr. Fletcher said grimly, "So how much did you bet, Feanor?"

"Everything. I had no choice. All the races and contests are now part of the new royal lottery. If you want the *grand* prize, you have to bet all you own—including your livelihood."

"What do you mean, 'your livelihood?'" asked Jacob worriedly.

"If you lose, you become an indentured servant of the kingdom for five years—to work for the king somewhere in the salt mines," answered Feanor sullenly. "Unless you can find some means to pay—and of course you can't. Even your home is gone."

"Not your house too!" Mrs. Fletcher cried. "Surely not that!"

"That too. Now that I've lost, they'll send me to the salt mines at Borea. And my poor family—they'll have to live in one of the shacks in the mine workers' village."

Josh had never seen such fear and disgust mingle in a person's face. Josh truly felt sorry for him. He knew that Feanor was a hardworking man and good to his family. But Jacob had once told Josh privately, "My friend is addicted to gambling. He just can't keep himself from betting on everything. I fear he is going to run into trouble someday."

Now Jacob began to try to comfort his friend. "Well, it is not yet the end of the world, Feanor."

"It is for me. I've worked for years to have a nice house and a nice life for my family. And now we will live in one of those shacks that don't even have running water. And you know what it's like in the salt mines, Jacob. All of us will work from sunup until after dark. I will hardly see my wife and children."

Josh sat watching the scene and listening. This was a side of Pleasure Island that he had not seen. After he and Mark went outside, he asked quietly, "Is it as bad as he makes it out to be?"

"Every bit as bad," Mark said grimly. "That's why I

hate gambling so much. It takes money away from people like Feanor and puts it into the pockets of the rich cheaters. Gambling addiction is like a disease. I've seen some people get addicted to wine and some to tobacco, but sometimes I think this gambling fever is as bad as anything else."

"Is this happening a lot on Pleasure Island, Mark?"

"Look around you," Mark said grimly. "Walk up and down the street. You'll find that almost every family has in it somebody that's gone crazy over gambling. Sometimes it's the whole family. We've had a half dozen friends who have had to go to the mines."

When Sarah stopped by the Fletchers' house, she found Josh still there. She was horrified to hear what had happened to Feanor. "Maybe you should talk to the prince," she suggested to Josh and Mark. "Perhaps he can do something."

"We might try that," Mark said. "Feanor is not a bad man. He's just weak in that area."

The boys put their heads together then and made plans to ask for the prince's help. But late that afternoon, Mark came back after running an errand, looking very upset and frowning.

His father asked at once, "What is it, son?"

"I knew it would come to this sooner or later. I just knew it. Now I understand what Feanor was talking about. Have you seen any of the posters about the very latest contest, Father?"

"No, I haven't been out today. What is it? A race between crickets this time?" Mr. Fletcher asked.

"This is serious, Father. Here—I ripped one down. I can't stand to even look at it." He threw a poster onto the table, and everyone crowded around to take a look.

Sarah read the announcement aloud. "'Fight for your fortune! Pit your athletic skills against the professionals for a king's fortune. Bet your life and win!'" She looked up from the poster then. "This is disgusting! It's like a bad dream."

"It's no dream," Mark said. "People are going crazy about it. They're talking about nothing else."

"Who are the people? What kind of men would risk their lives and their futures on a foolish thing like this!" Jacob exclaimed.

"Poor people, mostly. But anyone at all who's addicted to gambling seems to be falling for it, too." Mark flung himself into a chair, saying grimly, "It's that Sylvan. That's who it is. He staged this thing as soon as they let him out of prison. He was the biggest criminal we had and a national embarrassment. But he's very good at fooling and cheating people. His contestants will be poor fellows who don't know a thing about his wily ways. Sylvan will make the contests look honest, but they will all be rigged for his people to win."

"And I fear this is just the beginning," Mr. Fletcher said grimly. "These games will only get worse."

"That's the way it is with things like this," Josh said thoughtfully. "Things start out maybe innocently enough—like a sport—and then it's not exciting enough. So people have to do bad things to make it more exciting."

"You are so right," Mark agreed. "In this case, they're not satisfied with just seeing a wrestling match. They want to be involved personally and make money for themselves by betting on how the match turns out."

The week was a nightmare for the Sleepers. It began with Josh calling them together for a meeting.

"You know we were sent here for a 'vacation,'" he said. "But I see now that Goél probably had more than vacation in mind."

"It looks like you're right," Sarah said. "Do you think we can do anything about all this gambling fever?"

"I don't know," Josh said, "but I hope so. It's bad stuff."

"You really think Goél sent us here because he knew all this was going to happen?" Reb asked.

"He told us the king had a weakness, remember? I don't know whether the king's weakness has something to do with gambling or not. But I do know what Goél would have us do if we can. And that's to give some relief to these poor people."

"All you hear about anymore is those 'You Bet Your Life' contests," Jake said in disgust.

Reb nodded. "I remember it was the same back before we came to Nuworld. Some people even started betting on the weather forecast."

"I know they did. And then there was the danger thing. Like in ski jumping. Some people were only interested in seeing a skier lose control and go rolling head over heels down the slope. There's just something in some people that wants to see things like that."

They talked much but came to no solution. When the first day of the contests came, most of the Sleepers wondered whether they should even go to the arena.

"Well, I've got to go whether I want to or not," Reb said. "I've agreed to ride a horse for the princess."

Sarah nodded unhappily. "I've got to go, too. They're having an archery contest before the big wrestling match. If it wasn't for that, I'd stay home. But I promised Her Majesty I'd go."

"We'll all go," Josh said. "We might as well see the worst of it."

The arena was packed. There appeared to be not an extra seat in the entire structure. People even stood in the aisles and around the top deck.

Reb spoke quietly to Lightning, who seemed to be more nervous than usual.

"It's all right, boy. All you have to do is run."

Prince Derek was standing close by. The two were not in the same race, but they stood together in the stalls, talking about the horses and their opponents.

Derek tilted his head. "Listen to that roar out there. They don't care at all that some people are about to be wiped out financially and forced to become slaves."

"It's a sad thing," Reb said. "When we first came to Pleasure Island, it seemed like a nice enough place. People seemed a little bit too frivolous maybe, but that's no crime."

"Things have changed, Reb," the prince said. "And it's getting worse all the time. I see where this idea of fun being everything can take over a country. It's not good."

Josh watched the events in the arena move along as the crowd cheered wildly. Reb won his race. So did the prince. Sarah took second in the archery contest. One poor man had chosen to wager for the grand archery prize. He lost and was carried off by the sheriff's men. His property was to be seized by the kingdom, and the man would become an indentured slave —in the royal salt mines.

And then the crowd in the stands began to scream, "Wrestle for the money! Wrestle for the money!"

Josh Adams and the other boys were sitting with the royal family and Abbey and Sarah in the king's box. Josh thought Sarah wore a sick expression on her face.

"Just listen to them," she said. "Just listen."

Abbey and Cosima just looked at her, seemingly a little surprised.

The princess said, "I think you don't understand, Sarah. If this man beats the professional wrestler Kapo, he'll get a fortune. He can live out his life in comfort and luxury."

"I don't care," Sarah said. "I don't care. Mark tells me that the poor fellow doesn't have a chance."

Abbey said nothing.

Then Kapo came into the arena and stood awaiting his opponent.

Princess Cosima rose and cried, "Crush him, Kapo!"

The huge wrestler looked up and grinned broadly. He raised his massive arm and called up to her, "I dedicate this victim to you, Princess."

"Oh, isn't that exciting!" Cosima said.

"Not very," Sarah answered coldly.

The gate opened, and another man came into the arena. He was small in contrast to Kapo, although he did look to be muscular and quick. He was smiling, just as Kapo was.

"What's he got to smile about?" Jake asked. He was sitting between Josh and Dave.

"He thinks he can win," Dave said. "I've heard all about him. He's won some local wrestling matches but never a match against a professional."

"He doesn't have any more chance than I do," Wash muttered. "Look at him. He's got nothing to take on Kapo. Unless he's a faster runner."

Josh thought that was probably true. The challenger was fit looking, but he possessed none of the muscle build of a professional such as Kapo. All he had was enthusiasm.

"He's a dead man," Jake said under his breath. "I feel sorry for the poor guy."

The contest began, and it was obvious at once that the challenger had some training.

For several minutes, Kapo seemed to be simply playing with the man, as if to make the match last longer and entertain the crowd. He even allowed the challenger to get in a few good holds, if only for a few seconds.

"Kapo's taking his time," the king said to his wife. "But he'll win. You'll see. He's a smart wrestler."

The queen said, "I suppose you're right, husband."

King Leo smiled at her. "Things will be so much better when you are on Soma," he said. "Then all we have to do is convince Derek to use it, and we'll be a happy, united family."

"Oh, I'm sure we will eventually," the queen said. But when Josh glanced at Tamsin, the queen's face was twisted and she was obviously trying to restrain herself from weeping.

The two opponents kept circling each other warily. Several times it appeared as though the challenger was about to spring toward Kapo. But each time, Kapo moved swiftly for such a huge man, and he refrained.

Finally, and almost with desperation, the smaller wrestler lunged for Kapo's feet, attempting to trip him. Kapo almost fell, but he rolled to one side so that the challenger himself hit the mat. Kapo sprang forward at once and pinned him down with his whole body. The referee made his count and declared Kapo the winner.

Even then, the giant seemed content to keep the beaten man pinned, as if to squeeze more than just his life savings out of him. But at last Kapo stood up.

He lifted his massive arm in a gesture of triumph, as the crowd roared. Then he grinned up at Cosima. "For you, my Princess!" he said.

The king was highly pleased with the victory. He had won a large wager, he said, not to mention another free laborer for the royal salt mines. As one of the servants ran to collect his winnings, the king turned toward Derek, who was standing silently over to one side, his face stiff.

"What's wrong with you, son?" he said. "Why do you have to be so standoffish? Why can't you join in with the fun?"

"You call it fun to see a helpless man crushed and made penniless?"

"Crushed?" Sudden rage seemed to come over the king. "A helpless man? We were giving him a chance to win a fortune!"

"He had no more chance of winning a fortune and freedom than I have of flying! If you were in your right mind, Father, you would know that!"

A shocked silence fell over the royal box, and Josh thought he saw Lady Maeve smiling behind her hand. Perhaps she was thinking that things were going exactly according to plan.

In any case, the king looked confused for a moment, and then his rage burst forth. "You've been spoiled! Well, there's an end to that! Leave the palace! Go out and make your own way! You'll come back!"

"You mean that, Father?"

"Do I mean it? I command it! Get out of my sight!"

Derek immediately stepped over and kissed his

mother. Then he turned and left the royal box without another word.

"Leo, call him back!" the queen cried.

"Call him back? He'll come back soon enough— and on his hands and knees."

"I believe you have done the right thing, Your Majesty," Lady Maeve said in a low voice. "Indeed, he needs to learn discipline."

Josh, who had been close enough to catch this, turned away, sickened. He told Sarah what he had overheard.

She said, "It's terrible, Josh. What will Derek ever do?"

"What will the country do with that woman in control? If she can cause the king to throw his only son out, what will happen next?"

10

The Chariot Race

Sarah noticed that the posters proclaiming the next "You Bet Your Life" wrestling match dominated the walls of all the buildings. Everywhere there were notices saying that the event would take place on the following day. All citizens were urged to come, and the odds of the challenger against the huge Kapo were posted.

Walking along and shaking her head with disgust, Sarah caught snatches of conversation from the people going by. All were talking about betting their life's fortune. She turned in at the palace gate, where she was greeted by the guard, who was familiar with all of the Sleepers by now. Looking across the green palace lawn, she saw Dave and Abbey in the distance, walking with the princess.

I might as well have another try, Sarah thought grimly. *It hasn't done any good so far. But one of them just might listen to reason.* As she hurried to catch up, she had little hope of Princess Cosima's listening. It was a different matter with Dave and Abbey, though, for the three of them had become very close. At times she and Josh would get very angry at the behavior of their two friends, but Sarah now thought, *It's just that they're not themselves. Both of them are very sweet people when they're not on that terrible drug. We've got to get them off of Soma somehow.*

"Hello, Sarah." Princess Cosima beamed at her. "Do you want to come with us?"

"Where are you going?" Sarah asked, falling into step with them.

"Abbey and I are going to buy new gowns for the ball that's after the wrestling match tomorrow. Dave is just keeping us company."

Sarah said nothing, and Cosima laughed a little. "I forgot. You don't care much about dresses. It's a good thing there are girls like Abbey and me in the world, or the dressmakers would go bankrupt."

Sarah said, "I don't really think I need to go shopping. But I do need to talk to you for a minute, Dave."

"Me!" he said with surprise. "OK. You girls go ahead. I'll meet you later."

As soon as Abbey and the princess left, Dave turned to Sarah and studied her face. "What did you want to talk to me about?" There was a defensive note in his voice. Indeed, he stood facing her as if he almost expected her to attack him.

But this, Sarah had discovered, was one result of taking Soma. Anytime anyone suggested stopping the use of the drug or even cutting back on it, the user became angry and defensive. So Sarah did not approach the subject directly. "We're not seeing much of you, Dave," she said.

"I've been busy."

Again the tone was brusque, and then he said shortly, "What is it you want to talk to me about?"

"Dave, I think you know," Sarah said with a sigh. "The rest of us are worried about you and Abbey. You've gotten yourselves hooked on this drug Soma."

"I don't want to hear any more about that, Sarah. You just don't understand." His face was angry. He tossed his head. His mouth drew into a tight line. Ordinarily Dave was the most cheerful and agreeable young man, but now he looked almost ready to strike her. "Mind your own business, Sarah!"

"Dave," Sarah said gently, "you *are* my business."

"What is that supposed to mean?"

"It means that we Sleepers are not just seven chance acquaintances. We've been put together for a purpose. Goél did it. We're a team. We're tied to each other, Dave, and what happens to one happens to all of us. So when we see you and Abbey becoming what you've become—"

"I don't know what that's supposed to mean, either. Becoming what we've become. You're not making sense, Sarah."

"Dave, you're throwing away everything that we were brought to Nuworld to do."

"I'm not hurting anyone!" Dave protested. "Just because Abbey and I are having a little fun, the rest of you want to change that. Well, I think we deserve some pleasure!"

"Don't you see what's happened to you, Dave?" Sarah asked sadly. She reached out to touch his arm, but he drew away sharply. "It may have been just fun at first, but what has it become?"

"And now what are you talking about?" he snapped.

"I'm talking about this insane betting. People are throwing away their entire lives."

"You just don't understand!"

"You think it will stop there, Dave?" Sarah said, her voice getting more steely. "Sooner or later you'll see the entire kingdom in debtors' prison—or as slaves in the salt mines."

For a moment Dave just looked back at her with disbelief on his face. Then he said, "You're totally crazy, Sarah! You know it couldn't come to that!"

"It could, and it will. You watch what I tell you. Dave, *please* listen to me—"

"I'm not listening to you anymore, Sarah! And don't ever come at me again with your sermons!"

Sarah watched him leave, and a sadness came into her heart. She had become very fond of Dave. He had gotten off into things before that were not exactly right, but this was surely the worst.

"We've got to do something to save him," Sarah murmured desperately. "He can't go on like this."

Sylvan sat studying Mark Fletcher's face. Then he grinned at the young wrestler. "And how does it feel to be rich and famous?"

Mark did not answer. He had fulfilled his duties by wrestling any man that Sylvan put against him. In every case he had been successful, but now he simply said, "I do what I'm told."

"That's good, because I've got a new order for you."

And now Mark studied the cunning face of Sylvan. "What is that?"

"You're going to be in the 'You Bet Your Life' wrestling match in two weeks."

"No, I'm not," Mark Fletcher said calmly but firmly.

Instantly all the good humor vanished from Sylvan's face. He came to his feet and lunged forward to tower over the young wrestler.

"You'll do what I tell you, or I'll turn you over to Kapo." Sylvan seemed to wait for Mark to respond, but the young man simply continued to look at him calmly. "Did you hear what I said?"

"I heard you, Sylvan. And I'm telling you that I won't do it. I agreed to serve the king, but I didn't agree to become part of this gambling fraud."

Rage filled Sylvan's face as though he would hurl himself at the younger man and throttle him. But something in Mark Fletcher's eyes must have stopped him. "We'll see about this!" he shouted. "We'll see! You'll obey—just like the others!"

"I'll obey as long as your orders don't cause me to go against my conscience."

"Conscience," Sylvan sneered. "What's that? Show it to me."

"You obviously have none, Sylvan," Mark said. "But some people do. I will not take part in the slave matches."

Sylvan snarled, "Get out of here!"

And as soon as Mark Fletcher left him, Sylvan went to find Lady Maeve. "We've got trouble, Maeve," he said.

"*Lady* Maeve to you!"

"Well, Lady Maeve then," Sylvan mumbled. "It's that wrestler the king likes so much."

"Fletcher? What's the matter with him?"

"He won't obey my orders to take part in the slave matches."

"And you don't like people who won't obey you, do you, Sylvan?"

Sylvan suddenly laughed. It was a cruel laugh. "No more than you do, Lady Maeve."

The woman's smile was cruel, too. "Both of us want our own way, and we shall have it, Sylvan. Don't worry about that young man. There are ways of forcing him to do what we wish. But that's not important right now."

She turned as though their brief meeting was over, but then she hesitated. "What new event do you have planned for the arena tomorrow? Something fresh and exciting, I hope."

Sylvan nodded and said eagerly, "Yes. I think you'll like this. Here's what I'm going to do . . ."

Sarah, Josh, Reb, and Wash were visiting the Fletchers. Like Sarah, Wash always enjoyed playing games with Lalita. The two of them were seated on the kitchen floor, and the little girl was laughing with delight. Sarah had been helping Lalita's mother with some sewing all afternoon. Now they were talking quietly, mostly about Mark.

Then Mrs. Fletcher said, "It's getting very late. The day is almost gone. You must all stay for dinner. Of course, the food here won't be as good as at the palace . . ."

"It'll be better than that, lady," Wash called out. "I get hungry for simple stuff. Some cornbread and beans."

"Well, that you shall have, friend Wash," Mrs. Fletcher said. "That is, if you know how to cook this . . . cornbread, Sarah."

"I'm a world-class cornbread cooker," Sarah said, and the two set to work preparing the evening meal.

By the time the food was ready, darkness had fallen. Mark and Reb came in, both filled with excitement after running their horses.

They all sat down to the late meal and were almost through when a knock at the door caused Jacob to look up. "Who could that be so late?" he muttered. "Come in," he called.

The door opened, and Feanor entered. He looked tired and worn. Sarah knew he had been working long hours. He must have just left the mines.

Mrs. Fletcher said at once, "Come and sit right down, Feanor. You need something to eat before you go home."

Feanor did sit down and eat, but there was obviously something on his mind.

Finally Mark said quietly, "What is it, Feanor? Are the children all right?"

"No, they're not all right!" Feanor said, his voice tight. "How can they be all right with me working in a place like the salt mines? And living in that shack we have to live in? It's for slaves."

"Now, we're working on paying off your debt and buying you out of there as soon as possible, Feanor," Jacob said quickly. "I've almost got you a job lined up, too. Then we can rent a house for you. Maybe not as nice as your old house but—"

"I won't need your help for that, friends, but I thank you all the same."

Everyone expressed surprise, and Mrs. Fletcher said, "Why not, Feanor?"

"You haven't heard about the latest contest in the arena?"

Mark stiffened and said, "You're not going to go up against that wrestler Kapo, are you? That would be hopeless, Feanor!"

"No, no. There's a new event taking place." Hope came into Feanor's voice, and his eyes brightened. "I would have no chance against Kapo. But in the new event, any man who will compete in the chariot races against the professionals can win one hundred pieces of gold. That would at least be enough to buy my house back and get my family out of our shack."

"But the chariot races!" Reb gasped. He had watched one of the chariot races. He had told the other

Sleepers how small a chance any amateur would have against a professional driver. "You can't do that, Feanor. You wouldn't stand a chance."

"Yes, I have a chance," Feanor insisted. "It may be small, but it is preferable to what we have now."

Sarah spoke up quickly. "Think of your family. What would happen if you were killed? Those races are dangerous."

"Nothing that's not happening to them right now," Feanor said bitterly. "They have nothing even while I'm alive. I do not worry about the danger. If I lose, then I go back to the mines, and they can be no worse off than they are now. But if I win, they at least can have a life again."

For the next half hour, everyone in the room tried to convince Feanor that he was being foolish, that he had no chance at all, that he was risking his life.

But Feanor was a stubborn man. He finally rose, saying, "I've made up my mind. As a matter of fact, I've already agreed with Sylvan. You'll see my name on the posters." He tried to smile and said, "I've got to get to my family now. I have little enough time with them." He left then, and silence fell over the room.

"It has come to this then," Jacob said sadly. "A good man like Feanor will be destroyed to please the betting lust of the crowd. I'm ready to leave this place, wife."

"So am I," Mrs. Fletcher said. "But where would we go?"

"Anywhere but here." He looked at Josh. "You must know someplace where we could go."

Josh thought for a moment and said, "Yes. We could probably help you, but what about your people? This is your land."

108

"No, it's the king's land, and you can see that he has put himself into the hands of a sorceress. That's what Lady Maeve is. She has bewitched him."

"I don't doubt but what you're right," Josh said. "And that is all the more reason why good men and good women should stay and help do the right thing."

Sarah saw at once that the arena was full, as usual. Many of the spectators probably knew Feanor. Some of them no doubt had tried to discourage him from taking part in the dangerous race. Others had come simply to see the spectacle.

Josh looked down over the rows of people below them and said, "There. I see Feanor's wife and his children."

Sarah looked to where he pointed and saw the woman. Her arm was around the smallest youngster, and the older children stood about her. "It's so sad," she whispered.

Abbey heard all this, and she too looked down at the little family. Apparently she could think of no way to defend what was happening. She moved away from Josh and Sarah and went to stand beside the princess.

"Have you heard anything from Derek yet?" Sarah asked Josh.

"No, and I can't imagine where he is. It's as if he's dropped off the face of the earth. I'm not sure he's even on the island anymore."

They spoke quietly of how brokenhearted the queen was. The king refused to have Derek's name even mentioned in the palace.

Josh said, "When a family breaks up, it's a sad thing."

They had no time to say more, for the event was about to start. Feanor came and kissed his wife and children, then placed a helmet on his head. He hopped onto the brightly painted wooden chariot, pulled by four horses. He straightened up and advanced the horses to the starting line. His competitor, a longtime professional, looked smugly at Feanor and laughed.

The king, as usual, was seated beside the queen, and Lady Maeve was to his left.

"Have you made a wager, Your Majesty?" Maeve asked.

"Certainly!"

"For the master or this Feanor?"

"For the master, of course."

"I think that was a wise bet. That fellow doesn't look very able to me."

The trumpet blew, and the race was on.

Each chariot would make ten laps around the oval track that encircled the inner arena. As in the wrestling matches, the amateur was allowed to gain a quick lead on the pro, and that tricked the crowd into thinking that victory for the nonprofessional was a realistic possibility. Feanor seemed delighted as he bolted out in front of the master. He was ahead by three lengths by the time they had completed the sixth lap.

"If Feanor can just keep up this pace for four more laps," Reb commented, "he'll beat the master yet."

But it was clear that Feanor had little skill. He even struggled to maintain control of the team at times. In fact, his chariot wove on and off the track.

By the ninth lap, the master was running alongside his challenger, and it appeared that Feanor began to panic. In the final lap, he suddenly lost control, and his chariot veered into the stands. It turned over and sent Feanor flying.

A thunderous cry went up as Feanor went down and the master crossed the finish line.

Sarah turned away, literally sickened. Unseeing, she bumped into Abbey and Princess Cosima. "Just let me get away," she said.

"Princess Cosima, that was awful!" Abbey could feel her face twisting as she tried not to cry.

The princess shrugged. "The man had a chance to win a lot of money," she said. "Besides, he is still alive!"

Indeed, Feanor was getting up slowly from the ground, but he was limping and was a mass of injuries.

"Alive, but he's destined to go back to the mines! And look at his family."

Unexpectedly, Princess Cosima turned to see. "Where?"

"Down there. See? Feanor will be back in the mines all day every day. It'll be almost as if their father and husband *is* actually dead."

Abbey saw Cosima hesitate. She knew that the princess was a thoughtless person, had been made selfish by her life, and perhaps the Soma drug had made her even more callous. Nevertheless, something in her must have stirred.

Cosima reached into the side of her robe and drew out a small leather bag. "There," she said, handing it to Abbey. "There are some gold pieces in there. It's not what he would have gotten had he won, but it will buy food for a long time. See that his family gets it."

"Oh, that's kind of you, Cosima!"

At once Abbey ran after Sarah and stopped her.

"Sarah! Look—the princess is giving this bag of gold to the family of the man who lost the race."

Sarah gazed at the bag for a long time. Then she reached out and took it. She said only, "I'll see that they get it."

"Wasn't that kind of the princess?"

"This gold doesn't cost her anything," Sarah said shortly. "Don't you see? She was involved in enslaving that man. Now she's trying to buy off her conscience by giving money."

"What are you talking about? She didn't enslave him!"

"Everyone who takes part in this betting system is guilty of enslaving him. The *spectators* are guilty. If they weren't here, it wouldn't take place. Don't you see that, Abbey?"

It was as though Abbey Roberts was hearing a voice from far away. She suddenly felt a weight of shame, and she dropped her head. She found she could barely speak. "I'm—I'm sorry, Sarah. I truly am."

"I know you are, Abbey. But you've got to get off this terrible drug, and we've got to get Dave off of it. There could be an awful time coming. We might be out in the arena ourselves someday."

"That would never happen!"

"Do you think Lady Maeve would stop at any-thing?"

Abigail could not answer. She shook her head and whispered again, "I'm sorry."

Suddenly Sarah said, "Come along, Abbey. I want you to meet the family of this man."

"No! I don't want to."

"I know you don't want to, but you need to."

The next few moments were as difficult for Abbey

as anything she had ever known. She could hardly bear to see the woman embracing her badly injured husband and their children standing about weeping. Then Lady Maeve's henchmen came to cart Feanor back to the mines. Abbey watched Sarah take the woman in her arms and whisper to her. She did not know what Sarah was saying, but the man's wife held onto Sarah tightly.

Abbey watched Sarah speak to each of the children and comfort them, and at that moment Abbey Roberts knew for certain that she had taken the wrong way.

As the two girls left, she said, "I need help, Sarah. And I know that I can't help myself."

"You've got friends, Abbey. We all love you. And where there's love, there's a way."

11
For Their Own Good

W hat do you think about these shoes, Abbey?"
Abbey looked over at Princess Cosima, who was
trying on a pair of pink slippers. They were pretty
enough, but Abbey's mind was somewhere else. "Very
nice," she said listlessly.

Cosima looked up, surprised. Obviously she was
expecting Abbey to show her usual excitement about
shoes. "What's the matter with you today?" she asked.
"Don't you realize we've got to get something to wear
for tonight?"

"I suppose so," Abbey said. "But I already have at
least twenty pairs of shoes."

"Twenty! That's nothing! Why, I have hundreds."

Abbey had been feeling somewhat guilty ever
since the defeat of Feanor in the arena. The princess
had put the chariot race out of her mind. She was sure
of that. The princess thought that the money she'd
given had solved the problem.

But Abbey had been unable to forget. She had also
skipped her dose of Soma yesterday and today, so perhaps she was thinking somewhat more clearly for that
reason. In a way, thinking about Feanor and his family
was very unpleasant, and she had been tempted to take
the drug. Soma helped to blot out unpleasantness.

"I've been thinking about the family of that poor
man that was beaten in the chariot race."

Princess Cosima looked up with surprise in her

eyes. "But don't you remember? I gave them enough gold to buy food for a long time."

Suddenly Abbey felt a wave of impatience with the princess. "That bag of gold won't buy the woman's husband out of the mines. And the children still won't have a father in the home."

Cosima blinked. "You're beginning to sound just like Derek," she said crossly. "You can't let yourself think of these things, Abbey."

"Why not? What's wrong with thinking about things like this? The woman and her children have to think about it."

"But, Abbey, you can't take the burdens of the whole world on your shoulders."

"No, and I never said I could," Abbey said slowly. She had been thinking much about her life since coming to Pleasure Island. It had been one continuous round of parties and balls and concerts. She saw that she had been so immersed in them that she had lost her mental balance for a while.

But now that the Soma was wearing off a little, she was beginning to feel terrible. Actually, memory of the grief on the faces of Feanor's wife and children had kept her awake last night. "I just can't stop thinking about that family," she said finally.

"Then we shall just give them more gold, if it's really bothering you. I can get it from Father."

Impatiently and rather sharply, Abbey said, "Do you think that will make them happy? Suppose your mother was sent to the mines. Would it make you happy if someone gave you another hundred pairs of shoes?"

Cosima gasped. "Why, I never heard of such a thing! Of course it wouldn't!"

"Then why do you think it would make that poor

woman happy to give her money? It won't bring her husband back. It won't bring the father back to those children."

Cosima seemed confused.

Abbey had grown very close to the princess during her brief stay on Pleasure Island. The two girls had similar tastes. Both liked excitement. Both liked pretty clothes. Both liked to be going somewhere all the time. She understood that Cosima was uncomfortable.

"I don't understand you when you talk like this," the princess said.

"Princess," Abbey said slowly, "doesn't it ever occur to you that there's more to life than having three hundred pairs of shoes?"

"What's *wrong* with having three hundred pairs of shoes?"

"For one thing, how many of them do you actually wear?" Abbey waited, and when the princess did not answer, she went on. "I can tell you. I've watched you. You buy them and put them on shelves, but you have about half a dozen favorites. The rest of them you never put on."

"That may be true enough, but what does it matter?"

"Have you ever stopped to consider, princess, that you might take the gold that you spend for shoes you never wear and do some good with it? Maybe for some family that is hungry."

"I don't know any hungry people."

"That's because you are surrounded by luxury. But the palace is not the real world, princess. There are people who are hungry out there and people who are grieving. And just the price of one pair of those shoes would make a poor family happy."

117

"All right, then. All right. I'll give you the money for a pair of shoes, and you go make somebody happy!" the princess snapped. She clearly did not like being rebuked. "And so we've settled that!" she said irritably. "I'll wear these pink slippers tonight. Now we'll pick out a pair for you . . ."

While Abbey went shopping for shoes with Princess Cosima, all the other Sleepers except for Dave gathered at the Fletcher house. Jacob himself had asked them to come.

When they were seated about the kitchen table, he said, "I've taken the money that the princess gave Feanor's family, and I've bought back the house that he lost gambling."

At that instant the door burst open, and Prince Derek came into the room. Everyone started to rise, but Derek said at once, "Don't get up. And what do you mean by 'the money the princess gave'?"

Before Mr. Fletcher could answer, Josh cried out, "Where have you been, Derek? We've looked everywhere for you."

"I had to get away and think for a while. But I heard about Feanor's losing the race." His jaw set, and he turned to his father. "What's this about my sister?"

Sarah spoke up quickly. "She felt bad about Feanor's family, so she gave some gold pieces to me to help."

"She did that?" Obviously Derek was astonished. "That's the first unselfish thing I've known Cosima to do in a long time."

"I think Abbey's having second thoughts, too, Derek," Sarah said. "And maybe she'll be of some help to your sister."

The prince looked at Jacob. "You bought their house back?"

"Yes, and now I'll be able to look after his wife and children. They're in the house now. I went out and brought them back from the mine workers' village." He shook his head. "They were in very poor condition."

"I know. I visited the mine workers' village one day," Derek said.

"The village! *You* went there?" Josh gasped.

"All my life I've heard about it, but it's off on the edge of nowhere. Still, I wanted to see for myself what was going on, and it is indeed terrible!"

The Sleepers all sat listening while the prince told about the dreadful living conditions, the lack of sanitation, and the lack of heat in the mine workers' shacks. "It's poverty at its very worst. The only thing worse is the mines of Borea themselves," he said. "And there's no sense in that. There's plenty to be had, and most of those people are decent enough. Their gambling took them there, and now they just need another chance."

"Are you thinking of doing something about it?" Josh said boldly.

Derek stared at Josh Adams. "I'd like to," he said. "And I'm going to try, but I don't have much hope of success."

"You never can tell until you try," Josh said.

"Right now, I want you all to go with me," Derek said suddenly.

"Where are you going?" Sarah sounded alarmed.

"The council meets in thirty minutes. I'm going to go and ask my father to put Lord Denning back on the council. I'm going to ask him to let me help the people at the village and in the mines. And I'm going to ask him to do something about the gambling fever that is ruining this island."

Everyone stared at the prince, and Reb said, "Well, ain't this a pretty come on!" He whistled under his breath. "The king's got quite a party going—only he just doesn't know it."

As usual, the members of the great council had little to say. Lady Maeve so controlled them by her powers that she was sure they would agree to whatever she suggested.

The king and the queen both sat for this meeting, but neither seemed particularly happy.

The meeting was almost over when suddenly the door opened, and a guard announced, "Prince Derek asks admittance to the Great Council, Your Majesty."

Immediately King Leo straightened up, and his dull eyes brightened. "Well," he said gruffly, "he's showing sense at last! He's come to ask for our pardon. Have him come in."

"Yes, Your Majesty."

The attendant disappeared, and the king nodded toward the queen. "I told you the boy would come to his senses."

Lady Maeve, however, was not so sure. She sat at the council table, her eyes narrowed, as the prince walked in. Then she saw several Seven Sleepers with him, and her mouth twisted.

Josh and the other Sleepers formed a solid rank behind the prince.

"Well, you've come to beg for forgiveness, I daresay," the king said. "Down on your knees, boy!"

"I will bow to Your Majesty. But no, I do not come

to ask for forgiveness," Derek said boldly. He did bow, then straightened up and said, "Your Majesty and Father, I've come to ask you for several favors."

"You ask favors!" Lady Maeve cried. "This is astonishing! You should be asking for forgiveness."

"Forgiveness for what?" the prince demanded. He put his eyes on the woman clothed in black, and their glances locked.

For a moment there was a struggle of wills, and Josh saw that it was Lady Maeve who dropped her eyes first.

"You have ruined this court, you have ruined my father, you have destroyed my family!" the prince said loudly. "You are an evil woman, and I will not rest as long as you are in this kingdom!"

"What are you talking about, boy?" the king exclaimed. "She has saved me from my depression."

"Better to be depressed than to lead a country down a trail of despair," the prince said.

The king gasped and sputtered but for a moment could not answer. No doubt he had never seen his son like this.

Josh—indeed, none of the Sleepers—had never seen the prince like this. He spoke loudly and clearly and showed no fear whatsoever. Finally he said, "I ask your forgiveness, Father, for nothing, because I have done nothing wrong. It grieves me to say it, but you have put the kingdom into the hands of a woman who has no love and no pity and no mercy."

"Your Majesty," Lady Maeve broke in smoothly. "The prince is not himself. He is obviously suffering under some sort of delusion."

"He's not under any delusion, Maeve," Josh said then and stepped forward. "I have seen your kind before. We serve the lord Goél. Who do you serve?"

Silence fell over the meeting room except for the gasp of the council members.

"Who do you serve?" Josh cried again. "You do not have to answer! You serve the Dark Lord! I have seen his mark on people before!"

"I wear no mark!" Maeve protested, her face pale.

"You do not wear an outward symbol, but I see it in your eyes. And your deeds are evil, even as his are evil. Your Majesty, you once were loyal to Goél. I beg you to rid yourself of this woman."

Instantly Lady Maeve stood. "The Seven Sleepers are enemies of the state, Your Majesty! They must be treated as such. Guards, get them out of the council room!"

The guards advanced at once, and the Sleepers were forced backward toward the door.

Now the queen stood. "Leo, stop them!"

King Leo stared at his wife and said, "What are you talking about, Tamsin?"

"The young man is right. This woman *is* evil."

At once Maeve stepped behind the king and touched his shoulder. "The queen is unwell also, sire," she said.

Something appeared to come over the king at that moment, and Sarah knew with sickening certainty that there was power in the woman's touch. She was able to control the king just by putting her hands on him.

"Have them all confined," Lady Maeve ordered.

The king tried to protest further, but he seemed helpless.

The Sleepers were herded outside.

Lady Maeve said when the Seven Sleepers were gone, "Your Majesty, I must ask you to retire. See that the queen is cared for in her room."

Queen Tamsin gave her husband a panic-stricken look but she had no time to argue. Two guards came to her at once and gently led her from the room.

As soon as the door was closed, Maeve said, "Your Majesty, it must be clear what we must do."

"What must we do?" the king asked. His face was confused and troubled. "I can't think clearly."

"Then I will think for you until your mind returns," Lady Maeve said smoothly. "The council and I have agreed that the queen and the prince must take medication."

"You mean Soma?"

"Yes. It is for their own good. They are troubled in spirit, and a heavy dose of Soma will take away their disturbances."

The members of the council gave each other wary looks. It was the first they had heard of such a scheme, but Lady Maeve well knew that no one dared challenge her.

The king bowed his head. He did not answer, and Lady Maeve took this for an affirmative. "It will be done then."

The prince had been taken out by other guards and confined in his rooms. He could not believe what had happened, and he walked back and forth trying to think of a way to get to his father.

Then the door opened, and he looked up to see Linor, one of the king's attendants and the prince's own dear friend.

"Linor, what's happening?"

"It's very bad, Your Majesty," Linor said, his face filled with pain. "Maeve has forced your father to agree that both you and your mother will be put on the drug Soma at once."

Derek stood stunned. At first he seemed unable to think clearly. But then an idea came. "Will you do me a very great favor?"

"Anything, my prince!"

"I want you to take a message for me. Carrying it may be dangerous, but I must ask you to do it."

The prince scribbled out a message as Linor watched.

Linor listened to his instructions and said, "At once, my prince."

"Use your best speed, Linor," the prince said desperately. "I do not think that woman will wait long to get her revenge on me."

12
Jacob Fletcher's Plan

The knock at the door was quiet but insistent. Josh looked up and said, "Reb, would you see who that is? Maybe it's Sarah."

Reb ambled to the door and opened it.

Looking past him, Josh saw a small man dressed in the uniform of the court. "I seek Joshua Adams," the man said quietly.

"Josh, a fellow wants to see you," Reb said. "Come on in."

Stepping inside, the man said at once, "My name is Linor."

"I've seen you before, Linor. You're an attendant of the king," Josh said. "Why do you want to see me?"

"I have a message for the Seven Sleepers . . . but I see only two here . . ."

"There are indeed five others. Obviously, they are not with us right now. What is your message?"

Taking a deep breath, Linor said, "I have been loyal to King Leo all my life. I have spent years serving him. And what I do now may seem wrong to some, but I feel I must do it."

"What is it, Linor?" Josh asked.

Reaching into an inner pocket, the man pulled out a folded slip of paper. "This message is from Prince Derek. He asked me to bring it to you."

"Being the prince's messenger could be a little dangerous these days. I hear he is not in good favor with the Lady Maeve."

"That sorceress!" Linor almost snarled with contempt. "She has brought nothing but disaster to our island."

Josh opened the paper and quickly read the message. Then he read it aloud:

"My father is under the domination of Maeve. She has persuaded him to force my mother and myself to take Soma. I do not know what to do. I am being closely guarded. If you can help me, please do so."

Then Josh said, "But this is terrible!" He felt appalled at what he'd read. "How did the prince find this out?"

"It was I who told him," Linor said defiantly.

"Linor," Josh said, "go back to the prince. Tell him we will help if we possibly can. Tell him not to give up hope."

"I will take your message—and I trust that the Seven Sleepers will be able to help not only the prince but our poor island."

As soon as Linor was gone, Josh said, "We've got to do something about this, Reb. But what?"

That began a discussion that lasted for more than an hour. It was interrupted when Mark Fletcher came in.

"What's going on?" he asked. Mark listened as Josh told him the problem and then asked, "So what are you going to do?"

"We don't have a clue," Josh said mournfully. "Not yet."

For a moment Mark stood there, his head down. Then he looked up, and a bright light came to his eyes. "I think I know someone who can help. Come with me."

"Where to?"

"To my father."

"How can your father help?" Jake asked as they hurried from the room.

"My grandfather was an herb master. He knew all about potions and drugs—things like that."

"Could your grandfather help us, do you think?"

"Alas, he is now dead, but he taught my father much. We will tell Father the problem."

Twenty minutes later, Jacob Fletcher was listening soberly as Josh explained. Jacob then read the letter from the prince. He studied it thoughtfully.

"Do you think you can help us, Mr. Fletcher?"

"There may be a way," he said slowly. "I cannot promise, but if you like, I will certainly do what I can."

"It had better be quick," Reb exclaimed. "If I know that slimy woman, she won't waste any time."

"Very well," Mark's father said. "I must see what herbs I have. And someone will then have to make his way in to the prince. I could never gain admittance."

Reb saw both guards examining him as he approached the palace gate. He supposed they had been ordered not to admit any of the Seven Sleepers.

As he had expected, one of them said gruffly, "You're not welcome here, Reb. Sorry."

"Why, I'm sorry to hear that, Hector," Reb said. "And I don't understand. The princess invited me."

"She did?"

"Why, sure," Reb said. Actually, he was not quite comfortable with this statement, though it was indeed true that she had, many times, told him to come whenever he pleased.

"In that case, I will accompany you. You understand, though, that you Sleepers are no longer in favor at court."

"I know. You're just doing your job, Hector," Reb said cheerfully.

"You keep watch," Hector said to the other guard. "I'll see what the princess says. Come along, Reb."

Reb followed the guard, whistling under his breath.

When Hector knocked at the princess's door, Cosima's voice called, "Who is it?"

"Hector, the guard, princess."

"What is it?"

"The Sleeper Reb is here. He says you want to see him."

"Oh yes! Of course."

The door opened, and Reb stepped inside. "Thanks, Hector. See you later."

As soon as the door closed behind him, Reb took a closer look at Cosima. Her eyes were unusually bright, and the first thing she said was something about his accompanying her to a concert.

Shaking his head, Reb said, "I've come to ask a favor of you this time, princess."

"Of me? Why, certainly. What can I do?"

"I need to see your brother."

Cosima's face fell. She whispered, "He's not in good favor with my father. As a matter of fact, he's being kept under guard—he's forbidden to leave his quarters."

"I know that," Reb said. "That's why I came to you."

"Why do you want to see him?" she asked curiously.

"I want to help him, princess," Reb said simply.

"Maybe you haven't noticed it, but your family is in big trouble."

Cosima's face suddenly crumpled. "I do know it," she wailed and began to weep. "Everything's gone wrong! It used to be so wonderful. But now Father and Mother aren't speaking to each other, Derek is held prisoner, and—oh, Reb, I just don't know what to do!" She threw herself at him.

Reb patted her shoulder awkwardly and let her have her cry. Then he said, "I know. Life gets kind of rough at times. But, princess, right now you have a chance to do something to help your dad, and your mother, and Derek maybe most of all."

"Are you going to try to get him out of the palace? To help him escape?" Cosima asked. "That would be impossible, Reb."

"No. Nothing like that. First, I just need to talk to him—alone."

"All right, then. I can help with that. I can take you to him. Come along."

Reb walked with the princess down the wide hallway.

When they got to Prince Derek's quarters, two armed guards were standing at the door.

"I'm sorry, princess. No one can go in," one of the guards said respectfully. "We've been given our orders."

"It's all right, Morgan. I can certainly talk to my own brother. You can check with the king if you like."

"Has Lady Maeve given you permission, then?"

Suddenly Cosima drew herself up. "Is Lady Maeve ruler of this kingdom? Am I not the princess? Must I speak to the king about your insolence?"

"Oh no," the guard said with a worried air. "No

insolence was intended. It's just—well, princess, truly we don't know who to obey anymore. Lady Maeve gives one order, and you give another. The entire guard is confused."

"It will be all right, Morgan," Cosima said kindly. "Just let Reb and me in. I'll make sure that you do not suffer for it."

The guards stepped aside, Cosima opened the door, and at once Derek was standing before them.

"You came, Reb," the prince said, when they had closed the door.

"Yep, I did." Reb then turned to Cosima. "You reckon you could get your mama to come, too?"

"My . . . mama?"

"Your mother, I mean."

"Of course. I'll get her at once."

As soon as the girl was gone, Derek said, "You got my message, then?"

"Sure. Linor brought it, and we have something we think might work."

"You have a plan?" Derek said, hope leaping to his eyes. "What is it?"

"Wait until your mother gets in here. I'll tell you both at the same time."

The queen's quarters were on the same floor, Reb knew, so he and Derek had only a short wait. Cosima came back with their mother almost at once. The door closed behind them, and Queen Tamsin stood with the princess as Reb delivered his news.

"Now, Miss Cosima, I know you're not going to like to hear this, but things are pretty bad."

"I know," Cosima said mournfully. "I know. But I don't know what to do. I don't know what's happened."

"Well, in the first place, you've got to face up to the

130

fact that it's that Soma that your father's been taking," Reb said. "It's had a bad effect on him."

"Truly, my husband is not himself, Reb," Queen Tamsin said.

"I know that, ma'am. And now we've heard that he's going to make you and the prince both take Soma."

"That in itself shows he's not himself," Derek said.

Cosima began to cry. "I wish that woman had never come."

"Well, if we do this right, she won't be here long," Reb said.

"But if she forces us to take that drug, we'll become slaves, just like Father!" Derek said.

"First, you have to agree to take the Soma."

"Take it!" the prince cried.

"Yep. But it won't hurt you." He reached into his inner pocket and took out a bottle. "Before you go to Lady Maeve to tell her you'll take Soma after all, drink two swallows of this. It will taste pretty bad, but get it down—both of you."

"But what is it?" Derek asked.

"It's something Mr. Fletcher came up with. He says it'll coat the inside of your stomachs so that the Soma won't take effect for a while."

"But what about when it does?"

"No problem. Get away by yourself as soon as you can," Reb told him, "and have yourself a nice throw up."

"Oh, I see! That way our bodies get rid of the drug before it has time to take effect. But what about when she wants us to take more later?"

"You'll just have to fool her. Take the drug from her and pretend to pour it into a glass of juice or something. But instead, just drop it on your sleeve. That's the best we could come up with. The main thing is, she's going to want to see you take it at least once."

"And what's the plan for action after that?"

"You'll have to keep Lady Maeve and the king both convinced that you're on the drug. That means acting real excited. Gambling a lot. Hollering a lot."

Cosima bowed her head. "Is that the way I've been behaving?" she murmured.

"I'm afraid it is, princess. And I want you to keep on doing the same thing. You've been on the drug, so they won't be watching you. You can just pretend to take it. Nobody will know."

"All right. I'll do it. Anything to get out of this nightmare," the princess said.

"And I will," the queen agreed.

"I've got to get away from here now," Reb said. "You all have it straight?"

"Yes. And I think the plan will work," Derek said. He reached out and took Reb's hand. "Thanks for your loyalty, Reb."

"Well, shoot." Reb grinned. "What are friends for?"

The whole council was present with Lady Maeve when Derek and his mother came before them. Derek thought he saw a look of triumph in the sorceress's eyes.

But she stared coldly at them. "And you are ready to show better judgment, Your Majesty? And you, Prince Derek?"

The queen only nodded. It was Derek who spoke. "It appears I have been wrong, and I am ready to make amends."

"And you are ready to take the medication?"

"Yes. Both of us have agreed that it's the only thing to do."

"Very well." There was triumph in Lady Maeve's voice as well as in her eyes. Then she glanced at the king, who was blankly looking at his wife and son. "You see, Your Majesty, I told you that they would come to their senses. Attendant, bring two cups of wine."

The servant quickly brought two goblets on a tray and offered them to Derek and the queen.

Lady Maeve approached, bearing the vial of Soma. "Hold up your cups," she ordered. When they both obeyed, she put four drops in each goblet.

"Is that not too much?" the king protested.

"They are in serious condition. They will require more, Your Majesty. Now, *drink.*"

Without hesitation both Derek and his mother drank the liquid. They put the cups on the tray, and this time Derek knew he saw triumph flashing in Lady Maeve's eyes.

The king arose then and came to them. He put his arms around the queen, and she embraced him. "I'm relieved, my dear," he said. Then he turned to Derek. "My son, I know this is hard. But you will see that it's for the best."

"Yes, Father," Derek said. "I am sure what we are doing is for the best."

"Now," Lady Maeve said, "you both will, perhaps, sit in on the council."

"As you wish, Lady Maeve."

They sat for some ten minutes as the council business went on. Then the queen said, "I really don't feel well."

"Mother, let me help you to your room."

"Come back as soon as you have done so, prince. I want you present," Maeve commanded.

"Certainly, Lady Maeve."

* * *

The prince helped his mother out of the council chamber, and Lady Maeve turned to the king. "Well, sire, as you see, it has all come to pass as I said."

"Yes. But I do wonder about the queen . . ."

"Soma is a powerful medication, and I gave her an extra dose. She will be all right."

Prince Derek returned five minutes later. His face was rather pale, but he took his seat without a word.

"And how is your mother, son?" the king asked anxiously.

Derek looked at his father. "She's fine now, sire," he said firmly.

"And you, prince. Do you not already feel somewhat affected by the drug?" the sorceress asked.

"I think things are looking better, and I must offer you my apologies, Lady Maeve."

Maeve's eyes glowed, and she leaned back in her chair. "Proceed with the business," she said.

13
Another Dungeon

The darkness of Lady Maeve's room was broken only by a beam of pale moonlight. It slanted down through a high window and laid a silvery square upon the wall just beyond the foot of her bed. Maeve was usually a sound sleeper, but tonight she had tossed and turned for some time.

Then, seemingly from somewhere far off, there came a voice that she recognized—and feared. She opened her eyes to narrow slits and saw a shape beginning to form on the silvery square just opposite her. At first there were merely shadows and lights that intersected each another. But soon it was as if she were seeing a face that was hidden behind a glass and underwater.

The familiar voice came again, and she heard her name being called—"Lady Maeve—awake!"

The Dark Lord! Maeve closed her eyes tightly, hoping that this would turn out to be a dream. She knew that there were times when the Dark Lord summoned his servants out of sound sleep into horrible assignments.

"Wake up!"

Swallowing hard, Lady Maeve forced herself to open her eyes again. The shadows flowed together until a set of piercing eyes appeared and then a cruel mouth, a pointed jaw. And finally the entire face of the Dark Lord was before her. She could not take her eyes away from it. She barely managed to say hoarsely, "Yes, my lord, I am here."

"You have done well—thus far."

Relief washed through Lady Maeve. She felt release from the coldness that had clamped around her heart like a steel fist. "Thank you, my lord," she said with more strength.

"The kingdom is now ours for the taking. Only one task remains."

"I think I can guess that, sire," Lady Maeve said. "You want the king put to death."

"No, I do not. Leave him in place. He's a weak fool and will do well enough for a figurehead. And now that his family is under control, you can handle them. You will be the real ruler of Pleasure Island—under my authority."

"As you wish, my lord." Exultation rushed through her. She knew she had just been given great power and wealth. "What is the task you mentioned, my lord?"

"The Seven Sleepers." A hint of rage tinged the voice that came to her. Fury was there that went beyond the bounds of human anger. "This time the Seven Sleepers must die!"

This did not trouble Lady Maeve. "Certainly, if that is your command, my lord."

"You must make it happen soon. They have escaped my grasp too many times already."

"Let your mind be at rest, my lord. Their days are over," she said proudly. "You may depend on it."

"I trust I may. For if you fail, Maeve, I am certain you would not enjoy the fate that I deal out to those who do not succeed."

"Never fear, my lord."

"I do not fear. It is you who should feel fear."

Some power reached out from the image of the Dark Lord then and grasped her in fiery waves. She cried aloud.

"Perhaps you will understand," the Dark Lord said, "that is a mere taste of what awaits you if the Sleepers escape this time."

Maeve could scarcely speak. "I—I will see to it myself. At once."

The image seemed to swim then. Its edges grew fuzzy and unclear. The eyes turned into black pools, and there was a whispering sound. When silence came, Maeve sat up in bed and stared at the wall. Nothing was there now, but she knew for a certainty that the message she had received was from the Dark Lord himself.

She threw on her robe and ran to the door. The guard outside turned to her, saying, "Yes, Lady Maeve?"

"Take twenty men. Arrest the Seven Sleepers. Throw them in the dungeon at once. If they escape, you will die."

The guard let out a gasp, and fear ran across his face. "Yes, Lady Maeve!" He whirled at once and began shouting orders.

The sorceress stepped back into her room. Her heart was beating fast. She saw that her hand was trembling also, and she marveled, whispering, "I used to think nothing in the world could cause that."

A faint sound of shouting came to Sarah. Then she awoke as the door to her room burst open with a crash.

"What—what is it?" she cried.

"Out of bed! You're under arrest by royal command!"

A guard grabbed her by the wrist and dragged her from the bed with merciless strength. "You'd better put on the warmest clothes you have." He grinned broadly. "The dungeons are pretty cold. You won't find the luxuries down there that you have in the palace."

"You must be wrong!" Sarah protested. "There's some mistake!"

"One more chance. Get dressed and *quiet!*"

Quickly Sarah put on the warmest clothes she had, including wool socks and a pair of half boots. They were the clothes that she had worn when she had arrived on Pleasure Island.

Then the guard shoved her down the hall, muttering, "Get going! Get going!"

Sarah saw that the rest of the Sleepers too were being herded out of their rooms.

In fact, Reb was scuffling with one of the guards. "I can walk! I can walk! I don't need your help!" He gave the guard a shove that sent the man reeling backward.

Instantly the guard behind Reb struck him over the head with the handle of his pike. Reb fell to the floor but was cruelly jerked to his feet at once. Two guards held him then, while the one he had struck slapped him several times across the face.

"We'll take the starch out of you!" the man said. "You may have been a star once, boy, but you're nothing but a prisoner now!"

There was no time for more talk. The seven were dragged outside and down the street to a square gray building three stories high. There were no windows in it, and the very blankness of it gave Sarah a chill.

Josh muttered to her, "I knew they'd get us sooner or later, but I thought we'd have some warning at least."

"Shut up, you!" a guard said and struck Josh across the back with his pike. The blow nearly knocked him down, and Sarah cried aloud.

Once inside the gray building, they were greeted

by a very broad man with a bald head and a pair of small, alert black eyes. "Take them down to the lower level!" he ordered.

"There could be some water in there," one of the guards warned.

"Good. It'll give them something to think about."

Guards marched the seven down two flights below ground level. Once there, their captors opened a massive iron door with a bar across it and shoved the Sleepers inside.

"Enjoy yourself. This is Pleasure Island, you know." The warden grinned, and the door clanged shut. "If any of these escape," he warned the guards, "it will be your heads for it. That's the word from Lady Maeve."

Grimly one of the four guards said, "They won't get out alive."

The dungeon, Sarah saw at once, was nothing more than a large bare room. It was illuminated only by one feeble lantern that barely broke through the darkness. There was no furniture. The beds were merely piles of smelly straw that had been thrown on the dirt floor.

Josh looked about him and took a deep breath. "Well," he said, "here we are, folks. In another dungeon."

Abbey began to cry. "What's happened? *Why* are we here?"

"I think we're just about to find out who your friend Lady Maeve really is," Josh said grimly.

Dave seemed struck speechless, and he wore a dazed expression. He stared around the dungeon. He went over to feel the cold and clammy wall. "I don't understand," he kept muttering.

"You'll understand a little bit better when that Soma wears off," Jake said grimly.

Dave looked around him—guiltily, Sarah thought. Then he sat down with his back against the stone wall. He drew up his feet and rested his head against his knees, saying no more.

The hours in the dungeon passed on leaden feet. Early in the morning and then twelve hours later, food was brought to them. It was almost inedible, but Josh encouraged everybody to eat, saying, "We don't know how long this will last, and we've got to keep our strength up."

Three days in the foul dungeon seemed to have drained the last of the Soma out of Dave's system. On the third day, he said he'd come to realize what a fool he had been. Then, with broken spirits, both Dave and Abbey apologized to the rest of the Sleepers.

"I don't know what it was that made me do it," Dave said mournfully. "I've just been a fool."

Abbey said much the same.

"We've all made fools of ourselves at one time or another," Josh told them. "But we've got to stick together now. This looks pretty bad."

The rattling of the cell door awoke Josh. He had been tossing restlessly anyway.

Then the door opened, and the warden himself entered. "Come along, all of you," the man said.

"Where are we going?" Josh asked as he stood to his feet. The rest of the Sleepers were scrambling up also. Dirty straw clung to their clothes. They brushed it out of their hair and waited for the warden's answer.

"You're going to have your trial today. Didn't you know?"

140

"Trial! What trial?" Josh cried. "Trial for what?"

"You're on trial for treason. Subversive activities. Trying to undermine the authority of the king. You can take your choice. Any one will do. But one thing's sure."

"What's that?" Reb said defiantly.

"You'll be found guilty. And that's not the only thing that's sure." The jailer laughed, and his stomach trembled like jelly. "I can pretty well guess what the penalty will be. You'll be thrown to the beasts in the arena."

The guards laughed cruelly at that and herded the Sleepers out of the dungeon. They were marched up and out of the prison, and the bright sunlight so blinded Josh that for a time he almost had to be led.

By the time they reached the palace, however, he found that his eyes had adjusted. "Aren't we going to be given a chance to clean up a little before the trial?" he asked.

"It won't matter much. You'll be back in the dungeon before you know it." The guard chuckled and winked at his companion. "He'll be dancing at the end of a rope soon, won't he now, Cletus?"

The Sleepers were prodded along, stumbling and guarded on all sides by armed men with swords drawn.

Josh thought, *No chance of a rescue here or of breaking away. No chance at all.*

The guards hurried them into a large room where the king sat on a throne. Standing slightly to his right was Lady Maeve. She was dressed in black, as always, and wore a silver tiara about her head. Her black eyes gleamed with triumph as she said, "Have the prisoners face the king."

The Sleepers were lined up before the throne, and

as Josh faced King Leo, he thought that the king looked confused.

"We will hear the charges read against the prisoners," Lady Maeve announced loudly.

An old man with a white beard and a voice that trembled read a long list of charges. None of them made any sense whatsoever to Josh, but at the end Lady Maeve turned to the council. She said, "These then are the charges. You have heard them. What is your verdict?"

"Wait a minute!" Josh said angrily. "We haven't had a chance to defend ourselves."

"Very well," Lady Maeve said. "Defend yourself."

But Josh looked into the cold eyes of the woman in black and knew that their case was hopeless. No matter what he said, he realized, there would be no mercy from the sorceress. So instead of trying to mount a defense, he said in a loud voice, "You may be victorious this day, Maeve, but Goél will defeat both you and the Dark Lord soon."

"We've heard enough of this nonsense! What is your verdict, council?"

An older member of the council stood. "We find all seven of these prisoners to be enemies of the state." He spoke in a formal voice as if he had memorized his speech.

"And what is the punishment?"

"We decree that they be executed by hanging."

"So be it."

"Just one minute, Lady Maeve."

A voice rang out in the courtroom, and Lady Maeve looked confused. "Who spoke?" she cried angrily.

"I, Prince Derek."

Every eye turned to the door, where indeed the

prince stood, confidently eyeing Lady Maeve. Then he walked toward the woman in black. When he was directly opposite her, Derek said, "You are a witch, Lady Maeve—a sorceress and a murderess!" He turned to the king then. "Your Majesty, I appeal to you not as a son to a father but as a subject to a ruler. Is it justice to condemn men and women without a fair trial?"

"They have had their trial!" Lady Maeve shouted. "Arrest him!"

"Yes. Arrest me and have me hanged, too. Will that please you, Father?"

King Leo got up. He seemed to be a broken man. He also appeared to Josh to be heavily drugged. He tried to speak, but his voice was thick. It seemed it was all he could do to stay on his feet.

"Your Majesty," Lady Maeve said quickly, "do not trouble yourself. Your son is ill. We will care for him now."

"Son . . ." the king began in a trembling voice.

But he had no chance to say more. At Lady Maeve's signal, guards hustled Derek out of the courtroom.

"Now," the sorceress said with relief in her voice, "I'll take care of Prince Derek."

She turned back to the Seven Sleepers then. "You have been found guilty of treason and will be executed! Take them away!"

Two guards escorted Prince Derek down the hall.

"Take me to my quarters," he told them.

The guards seemed uncertain, and Derek understood. This was the prince of the realm, and yet he had been condemned by Lady Maeve. And everyone knew what happened to those who opposed her will . . .

With some relief, one of the guards said, "That's what we will do—for now. We will take you to your rooms. We will be forced to lock you in, though."

"That's fine with me."

As soon as the guards had shut the door, Derek ran to his bed. Reaching under it, he pulled out the length of rope that he had put there for this very occasion. Next, he tied it firmly to a massive bedpost, dropped the coil out the window, and looked down. It was three stories to the ground, but Derek was strong and athletic. Quickly he lowered himself, hand over hand. It appeared that no one saw him.

He turned to look back at the castle one more time before leaving the grounds. "Lady Maeve, you haven't won yet."

When Lady Maeve learned of Derek's escape, she screamed. "Kill the guards that let him escape! Kill their families! Kill their servants!" For a time, she seemed to lose all sense of reason.

She finally brought herself under control, however. "He can't go far," she muttered, clenching her fists. "He's on this island somewhere, and at least we still have the Seven Sleepers." She called a guard. "The dungeon where the Sleepers are—have it kept guarded day and night. Use every man you have."

"Yes, Lady Maeve. It shall be done."

"Now we shall see. These Sleepers may have escaped others, but they will not escape Lady Maeve and the hangman's noose."

14
Two Princes Meet

King Leo was slumped in a chair in the royal chambers when Lady Maeve came in.

"I am sorry to inform you, my lord, that your son has escaped."

The king hung his head sadly. "I can't believe all this is happening," he muttered.

"It is indeed grievous, Your Majesty," Lady Maeve said smoothly. "But we will hope to capture him. If the prince would only submit himself to my care, I'm sure I could help him."

At that moment Cosima appeared at the door. She appeared to be highly upset. "Father, have you heard?" she cried. "They've made a *criminal* out of Derek."

"No, no, you don't understand, my dear," the king said heavily.

"I understand that Derek is no traitor. He loves you, Father. Don't you know that?"

Quickly Lady Maeve stepped to the princess's side. "I'm afraid these things are too difficult for you, my dear. Come along with me. I think there is a ball planned."

"I'm not interested in a ball!"

The queen arose then and went to her daughter, saying, "It will be all right. Come with me, Cosima."

"But, Mother, don't you understand? They have orders to *kill* Derek if they find him!"

The king stirred himself, and his eyes went wide. "That is not true!"

"It *is* true!" the princess said. "Ask *her*. She gave the orders." Cosima pointed dramatically at Maeve.

"There is a misunderstanding here, Your Majesty," Lady Maeve said.

But for the moment the king had been shocked free from the daze that the drug Soma had brought on him. He glared at her.

Lady Maeve must have seen the anger in his eyes. "I will go at once and make certain," she said.

"Make sure that it's clear. For if my son dies, then you will answer for it!"

Maeve bowed before him. "I will see to it at once, Your Majesty."

As soon as the woman left, Cosima said, "Father, something's terribly wrong."

"I know. I know. The world is falling to pieces about us."

Cosima and the queen knelt side by side before him. "Please don't take any more of the medication that woman gives you," Cosima begged. "I have learned. It does make a person feel wonderful for a while. But then one behaves so . . . so foolishly."

Quietly the queen said, "I think our daughter is right, Leo."

The king sighed heavily. "You both may be right," he said and saw them exchange glances.

"All will be well, my dear," the queen said. "The Seven Sleepers say Goél has never failed them and that he will not this time."

Deep in the dungeon, Josh and the rest were listening to Reb tell about a hunting dog that he once owned back in Oldworld.

"That dog could track anything," Reb said brightly.

The light of the lantern threw its yellow beams across his face. Like the others, he was whittled down by the lack of food and fresh air, but he still had a cheerful spirit. "One time he tracked a pack of ducks across the sky. I shot enough ducks that day to feed the whole town."

Wash managed a little laugh. "That was some dog."

Reb looked around at all the sad faces. "We've got to pull ourselves together, folks," he said. "It's never over till it's over."

Josh grinned feebly. "You've got a good way of looking at things, Reb, but we're in a mess this time for sure."

"We've been there before," Reb agreed. "We'll get out of this one. Goél will do something. He hasn't let us down yet. You wait and see."

Sarah was sitting close to Josh later on, and she said, "Reb has such a good attitude."

"Better than mine. I'm supposed to be a leader, and here is Reb, having to cheer me up."

"We all need cheering up at one time or another. But Reb's right. We haven't seen yet what Goél will do. He'll get us out of this fix somehow."

"And I keep thinking that maybe he won't," Josh muttered. "As far as Goél knows, we're here enjoying a vacation."

"I think he knows more than that, Josh."

"You're right, of course," Josh admitted. "I heard once how somebody defined faith. The man said, 'Faith is trusting somebody so much that you believe a thing is so when your head tells you it ain't.'"

Sarah giggled and pinched him. "That's as good a definition as I ever heard. Now, see if you can sleep awhile."

* * *

Derek knew part of Pleasure Island very well. Other parts of it were not so well fixed in his memory. While in the city, he managed to hide himself by dodging through alleyways, but he narrowly escaped capture. Desperation came over him. "The guards are out," he muttered. "And if they find me, that's all of it."

Then he thought, *If I could just get out into the country, I'd have a better chance.* He thought about getting his horse, Thunder, but that would make him very conspicuous. Practically everyone on the island knew Thunder, and he would be spotted at once.

Another problem was his clothing. He was wearing princely silk garments, and he knew that was a dead giveaway. He passed by a poor man's cottage where clothes were hanging on a line. Fortunately one of the dwellers seemed to be about his size, so he took them, leaving five pieces of gold on a stone in exchange.

I doubt they'll report that to the authorities, he thought grimly. He ducked into the bushes, put on the worn and faded garments, and hid his own. Fortunately, a floppy hat had been airing on the line, and that would help conceal his face.

By nightfall he had made his way into open country, and he felt safer. Then he began hearing the roar of the sea, and he went down to the beach. Here he could walk and think, he decided, but all his thinking seemed to produce nothing.

A full moon cast its beams down on the green waters. It made the wedge-shaped pattern that Derek's people had always called the Whale's Way. For a long time he walked along the shore and finally realized that he was cold and hungry. He began to look for shelter.

He was afraid to go to any home. He was quite sure that there was a reward out for his arrest. But then he came to a farm with a deserted shed. Half of the roof had fallen in, but at least the place would give him shelter while he slept.

Derek went inside, wishing he had thought to bring food, but he had been thinking of other things.

For a long time he lay awake in the moonlit shed. His mind ran to and fro as he tried to come up with a way to help the Seven Sleepers. "They'll be executed," he muttered. "There's no way out. Maeve will kill them in the arena, no doubt."

Finally sleep did come, and he slept fitfully for some time. He never knew exactly how long, but he did know that he came awake suddenly.

Someone is in the shed with me! Derek grasped the sword lying at his side and sprang to his feet. "Who are you?" he demanded.

"A friend."

Derek did not believe this for a moment. By the bright moonlight flooding through the broken roof, he saw a man standing across from him. It frightened him that he had not heard the man come in. *He could have killed me while I was asleep!* he thought wildly. "Who are you?" he repeated.

"I have many names. But I know your name. You are Prince Derek."

"If you're out to get the reward, I warn you I won't be taken alive."

"Perhaps—if you would put your sword down— we might talk." The voice was calm and moderate and somehow warm.

But Derek was still distrustful. "Why should I talk to you?" he asked.

"Because, my son, you need a friend."

The words "my son" struck a chord in Derek. He could not tell why, but somehow he knew that this man indeed was not an enemy. He sheathed his sword and said, "If you know me, then you know that there's a price on my head."

"I'm aware of that. The whole island is being scoured, looking for you."

Derek slumped back against the wall. He could not think of a single encouraging thing. "Everything's gone wrong," he groaned. "Everything."

"When that happens to us—I've always believed—then our faith has an opportunity to grow."

Derek listened as the stranger began to talk.

"You see," the man said, "faith trusts in spite of circumstances. When the sun is shining, any fool can believe that all will be well. But when the clouds are over us, that's another matter."

"You're right about that, whoever you are. But my faith's not getting bigger. It's getting smaller. Besides, I don't know who to trust." Derek groaned. "You just don't know what's been going on here."

"I know a little about it. I know your father," the stranger said.

"You know my father, the king?"

"Very well. And your mother too."

"Who *are* you?" Derek demanded. "Tell me your name!"

"My name is Goél."

A chill ran over the prince. It was not a chill of fear or disgust but rather of joy. He had heard his parents speak of Goél and the wonderful things he had done in other parts of Nuworld. Derek eagerly stepped toward him. "Goél, have you come to help me and my family?"

"I would always like to think that I give help when I can. I am one you can safely trust."

"Then you can save this kingdom. It's gone mad!"

"Tell me about it," Goél said. "Leave nothing out."

For a long time Derek poured out his story. He indeed left nothing out. When he was through, he said, "That woman is a witch, Goél. A sorceress. I don't know what else she is, but she holds some power over my father."

"I have known Lady Maeve for a long time but have never heard anything good of her behavior. No, she is a servant of the Dark Lord," Goél said sadly. "She had great potential, but she turned herself over to him, body and soul."

"Is there nothing that can be done? The Seven Sleepers will die, Goél! And I know they are your friends."

"They are indeed. And so are you, Prince Derek, if you would have me."

"If I will have *you?*" Suddenly Derek knew that this was somehow a turning point in his life. Everything seemed to stop. And as he looked into the face of Goél, he saw indeed someone to believe in. He fell on his knees and bowed his head. "I am yours, sire, if you will have *me.*"

The hand of Goél touched Derek's head and remained there.

Time ran on, and Derek felt all doubts leaving him. Strength and courage began to build. When the hand was removed, he came to his feet. "Command me, sire!" he cried eagerly. "Anything!"

"You must rally your people, Prince Derek."

"They will not listen to me."

"You are the prince," Goél said sternly. He smiled

then and added, "I too am a prince, so I know the power that lies in you."

"Then tell me exactly what to do, and I will do it," Derek promised.

Goél began to tell him, and the prince, who felt he had suddenly grown up to be a man, listened eagerly.

15

The Arena

Abigail was sobbing softly, hoping that no one would hear her. She and Sarah had been given one corner of the dungeon, where they could have some privacy. Three days had passed since the sentence of death had been pronounced upon them, and Abbey felt at the end of herself emotionally.

"Now, Abbey, don't cry."

Abbey felt an arm slip around her shoulder, and she looked up. Sarah had come to sit down beside her. Just the warmth of Sarah's arm made her feel better. With tears running down her cheeks, Abbey said, "I've made such a mess of things, Sarah!"

"That's all over now. You made a mistake, but when you make a mistake and apologize, you don't make another one by reminding yourself of it."

"How can I help it? I was so foolish to believe in Maeve and to take that awful drug!"

Sarah squeezed the smaller girl's shoulders. "No one is holding that against you except yourself, Abbey," she said quietly. "It's time to put it behind you. You said you were sorry, and we've forgiven you, and that's all anyone can ever do. So no more tears."

Abbey wiped her face with a soiled handkerchief and tried to smile. "You always make me feel better, Sarah." She looked around then at the still-sleeping forms of the boys. "It'll be today, won't it?"

"Yes, I think it will."

"And you aren't afraid, are you, Sarah?"

"Yes. I am."

The answer surprised Abbey. "You are? I can't believe it!"

"Why should it surprise you that I'm afraid? You don't think I'm Supergirl, do you? We're all afraid. Even Reb. Just ask him."

"He doesn't show it. *You* don't show it."

"Well, that's part of a person's training, I guess. Learning not to give way to your fears outwardly. So don't feel that you're the only one that's thought about that arena and what will be waiting for us there."

"Dave feels worse than I do about getting everyone into this—if feeling worse is possible."

"I know. But Josh has talked to him, and I'm sure he'll get over it. So will you."

"I'm not sure we'll have time. Before this, Goél always appeared to one of us and helped us. But he hasn't come this time. He hasn't come!"

"It's never too late for Goél to act, Abbey," Sarah said, apparently with as much strength as she could put into her voice. "And now try to get a little sleep."

Josh was exhausted, and he knew the other Sleepers all were as well. They had been given somewhat better food recently, but life in the dungeon wore one down. Living in half-darkness, in a horrible setting, was part of the punishment that Maeve wanted them to know. He was sure of that. *She won't get me down though*, he thought with determination. *I'm not giving up.*

Time wore on, and the Sleepers had no way of knowing whether it was light or dark outside. Their watches had been taken from them, and, without sight of sun or moon, all times were the same in the gloomy prison.

Finally Josh heard the sound of many footsteps coming.

"All right," he said, getting to his feet. "I think this is it. Remember now, we may be afraid, but we can't let any of these people see it."

"Right you are," Reb said. "Keep a stiff upper lip."

The door clanged open, and the warden announced, "Came to bid farewell to all of you. We won't be seeing you again here. Have a nice time in the arena."

"We've enjoyed our stay," Josh said pleasantly. "Thank you for your hospitality."

"Yes, the food has been excellent," Sarah said. She gave the warden a forced smile and added, "We'll be sure to recommend your place to anyone looking for lodging."

The warden's face froze, and then anger burst out of him. "Go ahead and joke! You'll be dead in an hour! Get them out of here!"

Josh guessed that it was late afternoon when the Sleepers were herded from the prison. The sun was low and the sky a red wafer. It blinded him as it had before. Like the other Sleepers, he kept his eyes covered as much as possible with his hands. The guards hurried them along, prodding them with the staff end of their pikes from time to time.

The streets, Josh saw, were lined with people who had come out of curiosity to watch them. However, many of them called out encouraging words.

"Don't let them get you down, Reb!" a voice cried out. "You rode worse horses than this one!"

"You're mighty right, friend," Reb said, waving his hand. "Thanks and just keep on cheering."

Some of the voices jeered, but not many. Josh

finally decided, *These are the poor people. They're on our side. They don't have any power, though, so they can't help us.*

And then he could tell they were approaching the arena, for he heard the muffled roar of many voices. Once there, they were driven inside, where they were marched into a large holding room.

As the guards locked the door behind them, Josh looked around him. The room was empty except for several coffins stacked in one corner. On one side were two great closed doors. From the other side of those doors sounded the roar of the crowd.

"Well, looks like we've reached the end of the line," Josh said. "And I want to say something—if this doesn't turn out right, knowing you guys has been about the greatest thing in my life."

"That goes for me too," Sarah said. "Why don't we all just say good-bye right now and tell each other what we feel—in case we don't have a chance to later."

"You think Goél won't come through for us this time?" Dave asked worriedly.

"I'm still hoping he will," Sarah said soberly. "We know he can. And if he does, someday we'll remember this and we'll smile. But I just want you to know, Dave—you're a great guy." Sarah went over to him then and, to Dave's obvious astonishment, hugged him hard. "I think you're wonderful!"

Dave swallowed. "I think you're wonderful, too, Sarah." He could hardly speak, but he returned the hug.

It was an emotional time for the Seven Sleepers. Beyond the great doors, the crowd shouted at some event that was going on, but they took this time to tell how they felt about each other.

Finally, Abbey, with tears in her eyes, said, "It's

156

strange, but I'm not so much afraid anymore. As long as we're all together—that helps."

At that moment the great doors slid apart, revealing steel bars. To one side was a single door, just large enough to allow a person to step through. All the Sleepers went at once to the bars and looked out into the arena.

There had been a wrestling contest, Josh saw. A badly beaten man was being carried off to the mines by Maeve's followers.

Ten minutes later, he saw Sylvan and Kapo coming toward the small door. Sylvan carried a key, and he allowed the wrestler to step into the holding room.

Kapo looked huge, as indeed he was, and he grinned evilly at the Sleepers. "Well, you've had your fun. Now you pay the piper. Did you see how I flattened that fellow that dared challenge me?"

Not one of the Sleepers answered him, and Kapo laughed. "Scared spitless, eh? Well, I'm a merciful man. I'm going to give you a chance to make a decision. Instead of hanging, you can try your luck with me. If one of you beats me, you can go free. If not, well . . ." Kapo motioned to the coffins piled in the corner.

"I'll take you on," Reb said quickly.

But Josh stepped in front of Reb, blocking him. "This is my time, Reb."

"Why, you little runt! You won't last ten seconds! All right, then. Get out there. Say your farewell speech to the king."

Sylvan swung open the door, and Josh stepped out into the arena.

He heard the screams and the cries that went up, but he paid no attention. Now that he was outside, he could see the hastily built gallows, with seven ominous nooses—nooses that awaited the Sleepers. He searched the crowd for a moment, hoping to catch a glimpse of some friendly face—Mark's, perhaps, or Mr. Fletcher's. He even had a vague hope of seeing Prince Derek. But no friendly faces were visible.

Then Josh walked across the arena toward the royal box, holding his head high. Glancing up, he saw that the king and the queen were both present today. He thought the queen looked distressed. He also saw Lady Maeve, her eyes fixed on him and that triumphant smile on her face. Behind the king and queen, Princess Cosima stood, and Josh could see that she was weeping. The crowd quieted down as he approached the royal box.

When he was close enough, Josh spoke. "We are no traitors to you, O King Leo. We came to bring peace to your country. The serpent that has stung you now sits by your side." Josh pointed directly at the sorceress, and his voice rose above the gasp from spectators close enough to hear. "Though I die today, your time comes quickly, Maeve. You and all followers of the Dark Lord will perish!"

Maeve turned pale and made a quick signal with her hand. Josh heard a nearby gate clang, and he whirled about to see Kapo striding toward him. The giant looked ready to wrestle, even ready to kill. The match was on.

Josh had wrestled before, but not against anyone of Kapo's size and skill. Another cry went up from the crowd, but Josh paid no heed. *I've got to use his size against him somehow*, he said to himself.

Perhaps the huge wrestler planned to crush his opponent in one mighty lunge, for Kapo did not hesitate. Laughing wickedly, he charged, more rapidly than

Josh would have thought possible for a man his size. Josh held his breath.

When Kapo was only a few feet away, Josh called out loudly, "For Goél and the House of Goél!"

Kapo was likely not expecting Josh to be as calm or as quick as he was. With one swift move, Josh deftly turned, allowing Kapo to race by him like a mad rhino. The force of the big wrestler's charge was too great to stop easily. Stunned by Josh's quick dodge, Kapo plunged toward the gallows built for the Seven Sleepers.

With a loud crash, his head and shoulders slammed into the central support post. The whole gallows shuddered with the mighty impact. Kapo, stopped in his tracks, collapsed like a rag doll at the foot of the gallows. As the stands of spectators watched in total silence, the whole gallows creaked and groaned, then collapsed itself, as formless as the giant wrestler.

With a yell, Josh ran to the pile of timbers, stood atop it, and cried, "For the House of Goél!"

The crowd began screaming, "The Sleeper! The Sleeper! He has won his freedom! Turn him loose!"

Sylvan watched Kapo's defeat from across the arena. It was obvious that Lady Maeve's plan had gone wrong. She had been sure none of the Sleepers could defeat her champion, but he knew the wily woman had a backup plan, anyway. Now she sent another signal, which he saw at once.

Throwing back the barred door, he leaped into the waiting area. He grabbed the two girls by the arm and thrust them out into the arena. "We can find another gallows," he grated. And his eyes narrowed as he eyed the tall poles that held torches for night events.

Then someone struck him in the back, hard, and he turned to see that it was Reb Jackson. He backhanded the boy and knocked him to the floor, where he lay shaking his head.

"All of you, get out there!" he ordered the boys. And he shoved each one through the doorway. Then Sylvan raced across the arena toward the collapsed gallows. No, the Seven Sleepers would not escape their fate of hanging.

Unbelieving, the king watched from the royal box. There were the Seven Sleepers, clustered together at the center of the arena. There was that deceiver Sylvan, gathering up the ropes from the fallen gallows. The king cried, "What *is* this? What is happening here?"

"They are traitors, my lord," Maeve said calmly. "The Seven Sleepers have been proven traitors."

At that moment a piercing shout suddenly rose above the din, and the king saw still another figure running into the arena and toward the Sleepers.

"Who is that? Who cries?" the king asked. This time he stood to his feet.

The newcomer stopped then, standing between the Seven Sleepers and the royal box. He wore a cloak with a hood, and his face was not visible. Voices everywhere were crying, "Who *is* that?"

The king again asked the woman beside him. "Who is that man, Lady Maeve? And what is going on here?"

Maeve tossed her head angrily. "I do not know, but he is a dead man."

Suddenly the man threw back the hood, and a shout sounded from the spectators.

"Prince Derek! It is the prince!"

And then the king seemed to freeze.

Queen Tamsin arose and took his arm. When he faced her, she said, "There is your brave son, Leo. He is risking his life to save those young people. Is that what you want? Your own son to die to give a thrill to a bloodthirsty crowd?"

The king reeled backward as though his wife had struck him. He stared wildly about the arena. He saw Sylvan and his men hurrying to rig ropes to the torch poles. Then he realized what they were doing. They were building a makeshift gallows. Suddenly he leaped to the edge of the royal box and shouted, "Stop! Stop the executions!"

Sylvan heard the king. But he also heard another voice as he pulled the last rope from the destroyed gallows. It was the terrible voice of Maeve, and she was screeching, *"Hang them, Sylvan! Hang them!"*

Sylvan and his guards finished attaching the ropes to the light poles. Seven nooses once again swung in the breeze. Then he cried, "Now, Sleepers, let's see what you can do with your necks stretched!"

16
Long Live the King!

When Sylvan heard Lady Maeve scream, "Hang them!" he nodded and shouted back, "They are dead!" As quickly as he could, he started toward the Seven Sleepers.

And then he saw that another figure was standing in front of them. Sylvan stared at the man in shock.

"Get out of the way, Mark," he growled, "unless you want to die, too!"

"You're not hanging anyone, Sylvan," Mark Fletcher said, and his face was deadly serious. "I've never wanted to hurt anyone, but you're not touching these youngsters."

"You've lived too long," Sylvan roared.

Sylvan himself had once wrestled. Without hesitating, he rushed at the youth. He launched a blow that would have stunned the young man so that his neck could be broken—if the blow had reached him.

But Mark Fletcher ducked, reached down swiftly, and seized Sylvan's leg. He twisted and lifted, and the con man rose in the air. He turned a complete somersault and landed on his back.

Sylvan leaped to his feet and snarled, "I'll kill you for that!"

Mark Fletcher waited, and the crowd waited, also. The arena was totally still.

Sylvan threw himself at Mark. His long arms went around the young wrestler, and he began bending him

163

backward. Mark reached around Sylvan and joined his own hands, and the two struggled.

Although he had never been a professional wrestler, Sylvan was incredibly strong. It was a struggle of Titans. He laughed wildly. "You're a dead man! I'll break your back!" He applied all his force, expecting the younger, smaller man to bend. To his shock he discovered that Mark Fletcher's body was like steel. Instead, the young wrestler's arms closed about him more tightly, and he was slowly bent backward himself. Sylvan struggled manfully and cried out. But only by a mighty wrench did he free himself.

He snatched a knife from his belt then, and the crowd screamed, "No fair! Bare hands! Bare hands!" But Sylvan paid them no heed.

His young opponent let Sylvan circle him warily. Then, when Sylvan drove forward, Mark Fletcher simply reached out, grabbed his wrist, and flipped the master of the royal lottery so that the knife fell to the ground.

"Leave, Sylvan, and save your life!" Mark cried out.

Stunned by the young man's strength and now defenseless, Sylvan turned and ran toward one of the exits.

As Sylvan fled, Lady Maeve rushed into the arena. "Hang those Sleepers!" she screamed at the guards.

"But, my lady," one protested, "the king has commanded that the executions be stopped."

Maeve whipped out a dagger. "I will personally slash your throat if you do not hang them! And the prince as well!"

The officer appeared shaken. He directed the other guards to seize and hang the Seven Sleepers.

Up in the royal box, Queen Tamsin cried, "Leo, they'll all be killed!"

The king was on his feet. He could hardly believe what was happening. "Save them!" he shouted. "Stop the executions! Somebody stop the executions!"

At his father's cry, Prince Derek looked up from the arena. "Do you want to see what your people are really like, Father?" Without waiting for an answer, he raised his fist and shouted to the stands, "Now, loyal subjects, protect your prince and the Seven Sleepers!"

Instantly the king of Pleasure Island was shocked to see men pouring out of the lower level of the arena. They came from every direction, and all appeared to be armed. Many carried bows, and these knelt in front of the king's son and the Sleepers to form a line of archers. To the rear were swordsmen, and on the flanks were spearmen.

"These are your loyal subjects, Father!" the prince called up to him.

Challenged by so many armed citizens, the guards withdrew. Derek was safe, and the captive Sleepers were free.

At that point Lady Maeve knew that all was lost. White-faced, she started toward the king's exit from the arena.

From behind her, Prince Derek cried out, "Guards, seize Lady Maeve!"

Maeve knew she had to get away quickly. She ran, pursued by Prince Derek's loyal guards. She had gotten only halfway to the exit when she let out a terrifying scream. She felt as if she had been placed in the grip of some giant invisible fist and was being squeezed to death. She squirmed, shrieking, "No, my lord, I have done my best!" Then she crumpled to the ground.

Stunned silence fell over the arena. The king left the royal box. He ran down into the arena and threw out his arms. "My son!" he said.

The two men met, and the king was weeping.

"I've been wrong! I've been blind! Whatever has happened to me?"

"You will be all right in time, Father."

King Leo straightened. He looked his son in the eye, and then he turned to the stands. He saw his wife smiling down at him, and he knew that he was about to do the right thing. He raised his hand and cried out in a loud voice, "I am no longer able to be your king! This is your king!" He reached back and drew Prince Derek forward. Now he held the prince's hand high in the air. "Long live the new king!" he shouted.

And the arena echoed with the cries of the people. "Long live the king! Long live King Derek!"

The Sleepers remained clustered in a small group. All were silent until Jake said, "Well, I didn't see Goél here anywhere, but somehow I have the idea he was behind all this."

"Long live the king," Josh said. "And Derek will be a good one."

The ship heeled over as its white sail caught the breeze. The water was green, almost emerald, and white clouds were undulating overhead, filling the blue sky with their bulk.

"This is sure the life," Reb said contentedly. He stood beside the jib sheet, holding onto one of the lines.

All the Sleepers were up in the bow, enjoying the warm sunshine and the breeze. It had been two weeks since the showdown in the arena, and they had sailed from Pleasure Island that morning. They had waited just long enough for the coronation of Derek, even though all had begged them to stay longer.

"Life will be different on Pleasure Island now," the new king had pleaded. "We need your help."

But Josh told him, "We must go. Goél always has other tasks for the Seven Sleepers to do."

As Josh glanced back in the direction of the island, now fading from view, he said idly, "You know what, Sarah?"

"What?" Sarah asked sleepily. She was sitting beside him, her back to the mast, and braiding her hair. The sun caught the blackness of it, and he said suddenly, "You have the prettiest black hair in the world!"

"Why, Josh, you never said that before!"

"Well, I'm not good at saying things like that."

"Why don't you write a poem about it?" she teased.

"Maybe I will."

"What were you going to say before you fell into raptures over my beautiful black hair?"

Josh gave a laugh. "I was thinking how glad I am to get away from Pleasure Island."

"So was I," Sarah said. "Life with nothing but pleasure sounds so good. But look at all the problems people brought on themselves when they tried to live that way."

"I know. And I'd like to do something easy now."

"Like what?"

167

"Oh, like fighting a T-rex or capturing a saber-toothed tiger alive. Something like that."

Sarah smiled and nodded. "I understand what you mean. Pleasure Island has been anything but a pleasure."

"I guess we've all learned that having fun shouldn't be the most important thing in the world." Then he looked a little anxious. "But we're not going to give up fun entirely, are we?"

"Indeed not. In fact, I'll race you up to the mainsail. The loser has to wash dishes after supper tonight."

Josh and Sarah ran to the mainmast and began climbing the shrouds. When they got to the top, they were swayed from side to side as the ship cut her way through the water. Both looked back then, just as the island disappeared into the mist.

Sarah sighed. "And now that Pleasure Island is out of the way," she said, "we can get on with other things. What do you suppose Goél has in mind for us next?"

Get swept away in the many Gilbert Morris Adventures available from Moody Press:

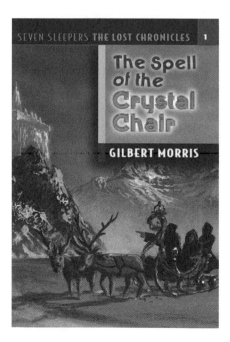

Dixie Morris Animal Adventures

3363-4 Dixie and Jumbo
3364-2 Dixie and Stripes
3365-0 Dixie and Dolly
3366-9 Dixie and Sandy
3367-7 Dixie and Ivan
3368-5 Dixie and Bandit
3369-3 Dixie and Champ
3370-7 Dixie and Perry
3371-5 Dixie and Blizzard
3382-3 Dixie and Flash

Follow the exciting adventures of this animal lover as she learns more of God and His character through her many adventures underneath the Big Top. Ages 9-14

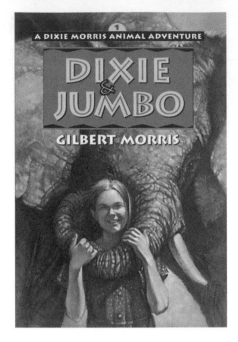

The Daystar Voyages

4102-X Secret of the Planet Makon
4106-8 Wizards of the Galaxy
4107-6 Escape From the Red Comet
4108-4 Dark Spell Over Morlandria
4109-2 Revenge of the Space Pirates
4110-6 Invasion of the Killer Locusts
4111-4 Dangers of the Rainbow Nebula
4112-2 The Frozen Space Pilot
4113-0 White Dragon of Sharnu
4114-9 Attack of the Denebian Starship

Join the crew of the Daystar as they traverse the wide expanse of space. Adventure and danger abound, but they learn time and again that God is truly the Master of the Universe. Ages 10-14

MOODY
The Name You Can Trust
1-800-678-8812 www.MoodyPress.org

Seven Sleepers Series

3681-1 Flight of the Eagles
3682-X The Gates of Neptune
3683-3 The Swords of Camelot
3684-6 The Caves That Time Forgot
3685-4 Winged Riders of the Desert
3686-2 Empress of the Underworld
3687-0 Voyage of the Dolphin
3691-9 Attack of the Amazons
3692-7 Escape with the Dream Maker
3693-5 The Final Kingdom

Go with Josh and his friends as they are sent by Goél, their spiritual leader, on dangerous and challenging voyages to conquer the forces of darkness in the new world. Ages 10-14

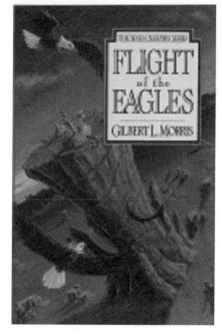

Bonnets and Bugles Series

0911-3 Drummer Boy at Bull Run
0912-1 Yankee Bells in Dixie
0913-X The Secret of Richmond Manor
0914-8 The Soldier Boy's Discovery
0915-6 Blockade Runner
0916-4 The Gallant Boys of Gettysburg
0917-2 The Battle of Lookout Mountain
0918-0 Encounter at Cold Harbor
0919-9 Fire Over Atlanta
0920-2 Bring the Boys Home

Follow good friends Leah Carter and Jeff Majors as they experience danger, intrigue, compassion, and love in these civil war adventures. Ages 10-14

MOODY
The Name You Can Trust
1-800-678-8812 www.MoodyPress.org

Moody Press, a ministry of Moody Bible Institute,
is designed for education, evangelization, and edification.
If we may assist you in knowing more about Christ
and the Christian life, please write us without obligation:
Moody Press, c/o MLM, Chicago, IL 60610.